ONE
OF THE
DEAD

Richard Farren Barber

Published by Crystal Lake Publishing
Tales from The Darkest Depths

Website: www.crystallakepub.com

Follow us on Amazon:

WELCOME
TO ANOTHER

CRYSTAL LAKE PUBLISHING
CREATION

Chapter 1

A security guard in a black uniform ushered a gang of teenagers away from the steps of the Council House. Their voices carried on the hot air as they complained about the disturbance. The air brakes of a municipal bus drowned out their protests. A man selling newspapers shouted out the headlines. From across the open space came the cry of kids splashing in the fountains. And the smell. Old blood, rotting skin and the hot breath of decay.

There was a flower stall on the other side of the pavement. Nick could make out the perfume of carnations and lilies, but the smell did not come from there.

Nick stopped mid-stride. It had been so long that Nick had forgotten to be afraid. He'd had months to lose the habit of checking the corners of every room he entered. Weeks when he no longer glanced behind him every few minutes as he walked along a street. Long enough to believe they had finally left him alone.

The stink was subtle, and it took him a moment to understand he was afraid. He searched the faces of the people who passed around him, but they were all busy on their phones or focused on getting to the next shop. He wanted to reach out and tap someone on the shoulder and ask, 'can you smell that?' He wanted someone to tell him that he wasn't the only person who could smell the graveyard stink drifting across the open square. But in that moment, he felt alone.

"Are you okay?"

He blinked at the woman. The face was familiar: brown eyes, pert nose, eyebrows knotted together in concern. He stomped down on the desire to scream at her that she needed to run – they all needed to run away – and instead he swallowed a deep breath.

Abby. The name unlocked a series of memories. He shook his head. *No, I'm not alright,* and then pushed away from her.

The stink of the dead man grew stronger. The throng of people pressed about him. He heard their breathing. Felt the press of their shoulders against his. They blocked his way. Slowed him down.

The man could be anywhere. Nick skipped backwards, almost tripping across a raised kerbstone as he fled. He held both hands out in front of him through sheer instinct and pushed aside a small child in a crimson school uniform. A teenager with a shaved head and a tattoo of a crucifix on her naked shoulder glared at Nick but stepped out of the way to let him pass. For a moment a gap opened and revealed grey stone slabs on the ground. Just for a second, and then the crowd spilled into the channel like water filling a trough.

On the spring breeze he caught the scent of dead flesh. It triggered images in his head of rotting skin dripping from broken bones. No amount of perfume could ever hide that stink.

Nick stepped into the road to escape the press of the crowd. There was no sign of the man yet. Vomit rose to the back of his throat, and it burned when he swallowed it back down.

Nick stopped. Hesitated. Changed direction. Followed the crack of brittle bones. It was the sound of wet skin, slick with melting fat. Nick had heard it a hundred times before and yet it still had the power to drive a punch to his throat.

"Nicholas!" Abby shouted at him. He reached out his hands to push her away.

She followed me? He was too focussed to do anything but note the surprise. All that mattered for now was that one of *them* was going to be here soon.

Sound beat against him. He closed his eyes and took a deep breath, drinking in the stench and the taste and the noise. Taking strength from the knowledge that he had been through this before and survived.

I need to get away, Nick thought. The rumble of voices was like static from an off-tune radio. Music bled from the open doors of a shoe shop, and it sounded like a woman's scream.

The smell caught him in the back of the throat. He gagged and swallowed down the taste of rancid flesh. He wiped the back of his hand across his mouth.

One of *them* was coming, and even though he should be used to it, the terror still overwhelmed him.

He staggered to the side of the street and pressed his hands against a stone colonnade, as if he was holding up the row of shops. Blank-faced mannequins stared out at him from large display windows. A canopy stretched above him, supported by a line of stone pillars. He could feel blood rushing through the veins in his skull. The cemetery stink blurred his vision. When he rubbed his hand across his eyes and looked again, he saw only the marketplace with people winding between the rows of stalls. They were oblivious to the danger as he ran amongst them, waving his arms to scatter them like pigeons.

The dead man stood on the far side of the square.

Nick recognised him immediately. The man dragged his left leg after him and his shoulder drooped. From here Nick could not see the state of the man's clothes – just a brown jacket and black trousers -- but he assumed that if he got close the man would look worn and bedraggled. Nick thought there was something wrong with the shape of his head.

He doesn't know I'm here, Nick thought, and relief washed through his body. He pressed more tightly to the stone pillar and stared at the man. It would all be over in a few minutes; Nick could start to forget what he had seen. Again. He was getting better at it.

He watched the man stagger between the crowds of Saturday morning shoppers. A few people seemed to veer away from the dead man, but most ignored him. He reached out a hand and brushed the white wire hair of an elderly man. There was no intent there, Nick could tell even from the distance. What would be the point? The old man would be good for one feed but nothing more. The dead man seemed to reach the same conclusion and continued walking.

Nick watched the elderly man as he pressed his way across the square. He bounced against the people around him as he stared into the screen of a phone *Do you know how close you came to dying?* Nick wondered, but he knew the answer already – the man was oblivious to what had happened. He paused at the edge of the pavement and glanced up before crossing the road and returning his attention to his screen.

Nick realised he had been distracted. He scanned the square but there was no sign of the dead man. People sat on benches eating their lunches. A bus idled at the side of the road. A teenager pushed a bright green trolley and held up a leaflet to the sky. "Have you been saved? Have you found Jesus?" he called. Nick whirled around, terrified the dead man had crept up behind him, but there was no one in the small space between the stone column and the glass shop fronts. Still, the sense of panic didn't fade. Nick pushed himself away from the stone pillar and ventured out into the square, actively looking for the dead man. He needed to know where he was if only to confirm he wasn't near him. He stepped off the pavement and into the road. When he reached the spot where he had last seen the man he could smell the stink – strong as poison, but although he made a full circle, he couldn't spot the man.

I should just leave now, Nick thought. *Put some distance between us.* That strategy had kept him safe every time before. The dead weren't looking for him; he just needed to keep out of their way during a hunt.

The chattering in his mind silenced. Every muscle in his body stilled. Nick listened, and once he was certain he knew where the sound was coming from, he opened his eyes and looked out across the square to the mouth of an alley. The black space was sandwiched between a newsagents and a cheap burger bar. The windows of the newsagents were covered in posters advertising lottery tickets and chocolate bars and headlines from the *The Post*. The burger bar looked like it had been closed for hygiene reasons.

Still, he remained standing in the middle of the square, scrutinising the faces of the people pressed around him and trying to spot someone who didn't belong there. He stepped onto a bench and used the height to peer above the heads of the crowd.

There he is.

There was a space around the dead man, as if people instinctively knew to stay away. Nick could see the thin strands of his hair laid across the bone white of his skull. He was walking toward the alley and Nick immediately felt a sense of relief. The danger was past. In another moment the man would be gone, and Nick could start the task of forgetting the incident had ever happened. It wasn't as if the dead man had even come close to him.

Maybe... Nick found himself thinking, but immediately rejected his mind's attempt to suggest the man was simply some unkempt guy. *I know what I saw,* Nick thought.

He noticed the woman, and it was like he could see a line tethering her to the dead man. She moved to the left and the dead man shifted his direction. She stepped into the street and fifteen paces later the dead man crossed over the same point.

He's going to feed on her, Nick thought. The knowledge was mundane, and yet, instead of walking away, he stepped down from the bench and headed in the same direction.

"Nicholas?"

He turned to discover Abby standing by his elbow. Her eyes were wide. "It's okay," he said and plunged into the crowd of people.

The dead man walked slowly, with a doggedness which suggested it might take him a minute, an hour, a day, or a week. The duration made no difference to him – he would get there eventually.

If she walks fast enough, she'll escape, Nick thought. She didn't need to be aware the man was following her; a brisk walk would take her away from him. Nick assumed the man would then turn around and pick someone else to feed off; there was enough prey in the city centre. Someone else would be claimed, but at least the woman would be safe.

When Nick emerged from the crowd the dead man was now only fifty feet in front of him.

The woman stopped to look into the window of a clothing store. The dead man stolidly walked towards her. Twenty feet. Fifteen feet. Ten feet.

Nick considered shouting to warn her.

She glanced over her shoulder but gave no indication she noticed the dead man. She could stare directly at him, and she wouldn't see the open wounds, the grey pallor, the grave dirt staining his skin. If she noticed him at all she would see the dishevelled state of his clothing and dismiss him from her thoughts.

Nick started to run, even as his mind told him not to get involved. *There's nothing you can do*, he warned himself. *You'll only get yourself hurt.*

He was twenty feet away from the dead man when the woman turned away from the shop window. She disappeared into the shadows of the small alleyway to her left. For a moment her silhouette lingered and then a small child moved to join her. Nick watched the two people come together in the neck of the avenue. The mother reached down and took the hand of her daughter.

The dead man shifted direction. Followed them.

Nick stopped ten feet short of the dark entrance to the alley. The woman was moving again. In a few minutes she would be beyond the reach of the dead man. That was all Nick could afford to care about; if he tried to take on responsibility for everyone in the city the burden would crush him, just as it had done to his father.

Still, he paused outside the entrance to the alley, unable to put the woman and her daughter out of his mind.

The alley was only slightly wider than his shoulders and the low arch scraped just above his head. *Any lower and I'd have to duck,* Nick thought.

The smell of decay was stronger. He hesitated. He didn't need to get involved. The dead man would find someone to feed on and then return to his lair. Nick wouldn't have to worry until the next time one of them came down to feed.

He halted, trapped in the liminal space between the dark alley and the bright city pavement. Here he was nothing. Invisible. Insubstantial.

He held his breath and stepped into the alley.

The brickwork had once been white, but was now a dirty grey, covered in black graffiti. He hurried down the short passage, afraid he was already too late. Beyond the arch he reached a courtyard with a huddle of old shops surrounding cracked paving slabs and a tub of dead weeds.

The man had his back to Nick. He wore a heavy wool coat, the material worn thin and covered with dried mud. Much of his skin was stained with green-grey mould and the side of his head was caved in, as if someone had taken a sledgehammer to his skull.

This time is going to be different, Nick promised himself. He felt the quickening of his breath; fear mixed with excitement.

It had been a long time since he had been so close to one of them. He had spent the last five years avoiding them and if anyone had asked what he was doing in the alley Nick would genuinely not have been able to explain his actions.

Because I <u>can</u> do something, Nick thought. *Maybe this time I can actually help.*

In front of the dead man the woman ambled, weighed down with three bags of shopping. She towed the young girl in the bright yellow dress after her. She was heading for a second archway at the far end of the alley.

As Nick passed the abandoned shops his reflection kept pace in the windows. He took a moment to ensure that he could see himself in the glass, which offered his only proof that he actually existed.

He stumbled over the uneven surface and even as he got close enough to touch them, the group failed to notice him.

The woman's daughter looked over her shoulder at the man behind her, but whatever she said to her mother went unheard.

Nick crossed the courtyard and pulled up before he crashed into the back of the dead man. He was close enough to see the individual hairs on the dead man's neck and each time Nick breathed he tasted grave dirt at the back of his throat.

How can I stop him? he wondered. He thought about pushing past and placing himself between the man and the family. Instead, he hung back from the confrontation, that streak of cowardice still not completely out of his system. He looked around for a weapon – maybe a length of old wood or even a brick that had come loose from the wall. There was nothing nearby. Just a concrete trough half-filled with grey dirt where there had once been flowers.

The dead man shuffled forward, gaining on the woman. His footsteps made a wet sound. He lurched, reached out and dragged his fingers across the young girl's neck.

Nick saw a grey stain blossom across her skin.

She dropped her mother's hand.

It was such a small thing. The girl flicked the back of her neck, as if attempting to swat a fly. Her mother turned to face the man and curled her lip in disgust. "Get away from us."

The dead man turned and stared at Nick with wet eyes. Three black teeth showed through a rip in his cheek. Greasy black liquid drooled from his mouth and ran down his chin. Maybe he wasn't really smiling. Maybe his rotting skin just made it look like a grin.

Nick took a step toward the dead man but then his own sense of self-preservation kicked in and he backed away. *It doesn't matter now, he's already fed*, Nick thought, but although the knowledge should have reassured him, he found himself doubting the lore that the dead could only feed from one person at a time. It was probably true, almost certainly true, but Nick didn't feel confident enough of the fact to bet his life upon it.

The dead man stood straighter now. The graveyard perfume of rotting meat was already weaker. When the corpse grinned, little teeth studded his gums; yellowed and crooked.

"Leave her alone," Nick called out. He was aware his words held no threat. He saw it in the dead man's eyes. The unspoken question was there – *what are you going to do?*

The woman turned in response to Nick's cry. The collection of bags in her arms rustled.

"You've got what you came for," Nick called.

The man smiled and then staggered after the mother. It took him two sluggish paces to catch up with them.

It's okay, he can't hurt you. But how truthful was that? The dead man had stolen the woman's child. Maybe it would take a year, possibly longer, but one day the woman would be alone. Could anyone argue that the dead man had not harmed the mother?

"Can't you take someone else?" Nick asked.

The dead man peered into his soul. The man sneered and Nick assumed his cowardice was as visible as the tattoo on his wrist. The man moved and the woman dropped her bags and raised a hand to bat him away.

She hesitated, glared at the dead man and then past him to Nick as if she held them both responsible for what had happened. *Maybe she's right,* Nick thought.

Beyond her the alleyway narrowed to the second exit. It was so close. Had she just carried on walking she would have been onto High Gate before the dead man caught them, and once there her daughter would have been safe. The realisation of how thin the line sometimes was between life and death struck Nick like a blade.

"I'll call the police," she warned them both.

She turned to walk away. Three steps and then she passed into the shadows beneath the archway.

The dead man did not move.

You've fed, Nick thought. *What more do you want?*

The girl coughed and brought her fist up to cover her mouth. Nick wondered if she knew she was already dying.

The woman stumbled. She looked at Nick, actually looked at him instead of through him.

"I'm sorry," Nick whispered. *I shouldn't have interfered.* The dead took what they wanted – that was how it always was. He was a fool to think he could ever change that.

The child slipped into the darkness and Nick was left alone with the dead man.

The egg-shaped outline of the man's head was fractured along one side. The crack spread along the skull beneath sparse hair. As Nick watched, the jagged line grew fainter. His skin began to change colour, from grey to an unnatural pink.

The man stood for a moment longer, and then headed toward the same exit the woman and child had taken, leaving Nick alone in the courtyard.

For a moment the world was still. Sounds from the city filtered into the alley but they belonged to a different world. Nick turned away and headed back toward the entrance. The narrow passageway was darker than before. A shadow blocked the exit. She stepped forward: Abby.

As she walked into the light he asked, "Why did you follow me?" He was almost at her side before he looked beyond her. Standing behind Abby was one of the dead.

CHAPTER 2

The man grinned as Nick approached. Liquid eyes stared out from sunken holes. He stood behind Abby, close enough to reach out and touch her.

"Nick..." Abby said. She turned around and found the man almost pressed against her and sighed in disgust. For one moment Nick thought she was going to push the man away. The warning was on his lips: 'Don't touch him!' but Abby stepped backwards and dismissed the man from her thoughts.

"What's wrong?" she asked.

The dead man's brown suit hung from his body, ragged and rotten. A tattered yellow tie hung around his throat like a noose. There were large holes in both of his knees as if the man had crawled out of his grave. His chin was covered in grey stubble and his skin had the dirty-brown tone of someone who had not washed in months.

Nick was grimly fascinated with the creature and he found himself staring at the exposed bone of his rotting jaw. He was sure Abby could not see this, just as he was sure the mother and daughter had not noticed the sunken skull of the man who had accosted them in the courtyard. If they had seen the truth they would have run.

The man took a step closer. A rip in the man's grey shirt revealed a thick slab of muscle from his stomach. "I don't have any change," Abby told him and turned back to face Nick.

The dead man raised a hand and casually brushed a strand of Abby's hair. The contact was slight, almost non-existent. Abby was oblivious to the man's touch.

Is that enough? Nick thought. *Isn't hair already dead?*

"Why did you run off?" Abby asked.

Nick shuffled forward. He was conscious that Abby stood between him and the dead man. He looked over his shoulder to the other exit from the courtyard.

"Abby," Nick said. He tried to lower his voice, to push out the fear so that all that remained was a soft, calm tone. Her eyes widened and Nick realised he had achieved the opposite effect.

He took another step back, deliberate this time, and beckoned Abby to follow. His outstretched hand trembled.

"Take my hand."

Abby's warm fingertips brushed against his palm. Her nails scratched his skin. He leaned forward to claim the remaining space between them.

Abby trembled. The dead man reached out and his blackened fingers caressed the very edge of Abby's hair. Nick felt his heartbeat quicken. He moved slightly forward.

"Don't touch her."

Nick checked behind him. The rest of the alley was empty. If he could get Abby away from the dead man, she would be safe. The girl was already claimed. He couldn't lose Abby too. He stared at her as if he could cause her to move just by willpower.

"Abby, you need to come with me."

"Why? What are you playing at?"

She took a step forward and the dead man followed.

Nick swallowed down on the need to scream at her: *Run! Just run!* because he didn't know how she would react. It was safer to ease her out of the situation, like walking a tightrope.

"Leave her alone," Nick said to the man. He blinked, and Nick had no doubt he understood.

"Leave off," Abby said, swatting her hand in the man's direction.

She moved forward and Nick flinched away from her. It was instinct, and as soon as he realised what he had done he felt shame wash over him. She wasn't infected.

"What's the matter?" Abby asked.

"Hurry up." Nick started to move. If he could get Abby to walk fast enough, they would be able to leave the dead man behind. The man had his pick of people in the town centre and as soon as Abby was gone he could prey on someone else. Nick wasn't proud of the thought – not after he had watched the girl become infected – but he needed to get Abby away. He couldn't save everyone.

The dead man stepped forward and placed his hand on Abby's shoulder. Claimed her.

His skin pressed against hers. Just for a moment, but when he removed his fingers there was a circle of small black marks on Abby's pale skin. They looked like fingertip bruises.

"Get off me," Abby said. She'd pushed the man away and stepped closer to Nick, all in a single fluid movement. Nick tried not to react, but he could feel the muscles in his legs pulled tight, ready to run.

"What's wrong with you?" Abby asked. Her voice sounded different. It wasn't anything Nick could explain. There was a low note to her words that hadn't been there previously, a gravel tone that reminded him of the elderly, the terminally ill.

He wanted to rush forward and fold her into his arms. His mind screamed out the warning, *she's infected!* Maybe he was wrong. Maybe it was just a test, a warning.

He took another step away from her.

Nick looked beyond Abby. The dead man was gone.

CHAPTER 3

"Wait here," Nick said.

He hesitated before he reached out and guided her to one side of the court-yard, away from the graffiti-smeared wall. The soft cotton of her shirt felt cool beneath his fingertips. He hated himself for being so careful. Abby raised her hands to push him away and Nick let go before she could make contact. "Just stay there, I'll explain."

He fled before she could argue. As he walked under the low archway and passed out of the courtyard the stink of stale urine burned at the back of his throat.

Shapes moved behind the glass of the burger bar. He imagined the two dead men hiding there, coming out to find their prey and then retreating to the safety of the restaurant. But then one of the people on the other side of the glass became clearer – a young Asian man, his chin speckled with acne. He wore a white and red chef's apron.

Nick passed out of the alley and stood in the centre of the pavement, buffeted by shoppers as they brushed past him.

He scanned the faces of the crowd. The dead man was already gone. Nick stumbled out of the throng of shoppers and onto the road. The sun poured down, too hot, too bright, and Nick held up his hand to shade his eyes. He glanced around him and hurried over to a bench outside Lloyds Bank. A woman sat, plastic carrier bags gathered around her ankles like a flock of sheep. Nick climbed onto the end of the bench.

"Get down. Seats are not for feet," the woman shouted. The way the woman spoke suggested she was reciting a sign. She repeated it: "Seats are not for feet," and her voice rose to a pitch that was almost panic.

From his vantage point Nick could see down the length of the pedestrian precinct, all the way along the side of the Council House to the bottom of Clumber Street where market traders hawked flowers and cheap cigarette lighters.

He closed his eyes. It was easier to concentrate that way. He heard the sound of feet dragging along the pavement and the chatter of voices. He heard the rush of water from the fountains on the other side of the square. He smelled the too-sweet aroma of burgers from the restaurant a little further down the road and even the sharp tang of bleach from the fountains.

He heard *him*. He heard his bones grind together as he walked. He smelled the graveyard odour that clung to him.

"I will find you," Nick whispered to himself. He jumped from the bench and started to run. He clawed his way between the mass of bodies, using his elbows to force a path through a pack of tourists in bright red jackets.

People stared at him, but that wasn't important. The only thing that mattered was finding the dead man and forcing him to return what he had stolen from Abby.

Nick barged up the street until he reached the corner of the Market Square. He peered through the crowds, hoping to spy the sluggish gait of one man kept apart from the rest, but all he saw were people packed tightly together. Chatting or arguing, walking hand in hand or linking arms. The sheer weight of bodies seemed impossible to navigate. The dead man was going to escape.

Stop it, Nick told himself. He forced himself to stand still even when the urge to keep running was overwhelming. He closed his eyes once more. Instead, he listened to the city centre around him; to the sound of people shouting and the rumble as a tram passed. Music drifted out through open shop doorways. He was buffeted by the constant contact of people brushing past him. He tasted sweet fried chicken and decay. Nick turned his head to try and locate the man. It wasn't possible to tell exactly where he was, but he could sense the general direction. He opened his eyes and struck out along the side of the Council House and when it intersected with the pedestrian precinct he turned left and headed up towards the Victoria Shopping Centre.

The flow of the crowd carried him like a grain of sand tossed into a fast-moving stream. He crossed the road in front of the shopping centre and for a moment considered going inside, but his instinct said the dead man had taken a different route. Nick pushed against the flow of people and went around the side.

He came out into an open space – an oasis in the middle of the frantic pile of bodies. He glanced around and then felt his stomach cramp with dread. The dead man shuffled along the pavement but even as Nick watched, his gait became even and his spine straightened. He smiled exposing those blackened teeth and rotting gums.

Nick ran at him.

The dead man held his ground. His clothes were as dirty as they had been before – one of the pockets on his coat was ripped and the lapel of his shirt was encrusted with blood, but the man himself had changed. Nick slowed to a walk. The man's hair was thicker; the white scalp no longer visible through thin, black wire. His face was flushed to a bright pink. The hole in his jawline had closed until it was now just a scar.

"Give it back," Nick said.

The man grinned. He stood a few paces in front of Nick. People did not give him a second glance as they passed by. It occurred to Nick to wonder how it must look – a man accosting one of the homeless.

"You can't have her."

The dead man laughed. The noise was low and ugly. It was more dismissive than anything he might have said. As if Nick's comment was so weak it didn't even deserve a reply. He pressed his lips together – bright pink, fat as slugs – and blew out a soft breath of air. It tasted of Abby.

Nick lurched forward but the dead man did not flinch, and before they came into contact Nick stopped. What could he do? Beat the man with his bare hands? He glanced at the crowd and wondered whether anyone would intervene.

"Give it back to her and I'll let you go."

The dead man blinked, a lazy, casual action that suggested Nick's threats meant nothing to him.

"What do you want?" Nick asked. The dead man appeared to consider the question. His wet eyes peered out from his broken face. His lips trembled.

Nick wondered what price was going to be demanded from him.

"I don't want to be alone," the man said. He turned and walked away before Nick could respond.

Come back, Nick thought. He stood for a moment in the centre of the pavement with the shoppers pressing against him on both sides. In seconds the mass of people folded around the dead man, and he was gone. *Don't touch him,* Nick thought. He wanted to scream it aloud. *Don't touch him.* He stood in silence for a moment, caught in indecision.

Somewhere behind him was Abby. Infected. He should return to her. Care for her.

Ahead was the dead man, walking away with Abby's life burning inside him.

He should go back, and yet instead he pushed his way through the crowd to follow the dead man.

CHAPTER 4

Cars and buses poisoned the air and poured grey and purple smoke into his lungs. Here the pavements were empty and many of the shops had whitewashed windows. Even the shops which were still doing business seemed abandoned.

The dead man walked slowly. There was an arrogance in his stride which suggested he had no reason to run. Nick considered picking up a metal bar and clubbing the man over the head, spilling his putrid brains on the pavement.

He caught up with the man at the kerb and waited for a stream of cars to pass. "Why do you do this?" Nick asked, although he already knew the answer. "Why can't you just stay dead?" He checked the man from the corner of his eye. Apart from his clothes, the man standing beside him could now pass for a worker on his way home from the office. He could be a teacher or a shop assistant. Nick glanced down; the dirt under the man's fingernails betrayed what he was.

"I'm not going to let you get away with this," Nick promised. "Even if I have to haunt you every day of your..." he hesitated. *Life?*

The traffic lights changed. The cars stopped and the dead man continued walking. Nick followed, almost at his shoulder now.

"You're a parasite."

The man made a great pretence not to hear, and Nick didn't blame him. He wondered how he would act if the roles were reversed – if he found himself needing to feed off others simply to survive. He wanted to believe he wouldn't do it, but he was afraid that he would be just as greedy as the man beside him.

"You've taken a feed. You don't need any more," Nick said. "Can't you find someone else?"

He waited for the dead man to respond. He still held onto the hope that maybe he could persuade him to spare Abby.

"There are so many others to choose from. Abby is just one person. Surely one life is as nourishing as the next?"

The man continued his slow, stolid walk up the hill. "Listen to me!" Nick said. "You can find someone else. Please. I promise I'll..." *What? Leave him alone?* The dead man did not act like someone who needed to bargain.

"I won't let you take her," Nick said.

The cemetery was at the top of the hill. A cast iron railing ran along three sides of the plot. A tall iron gate, thick with years of dust overpainted with coats of black paint, sat at an angle on the corner.

The dead man walked up to the gate. Under his feet the smooth tarmac changed to cobblestones, and he lurched to one side. His ankles flexed. Rubber bones that bent in an unnatural way were the only sign the man was not simply visiting a grave.

Nick halted at the entrance, unable to step inside.

The dead man passed beyond the gates while Nick stood screaming at him through the railings. He grasped the bars tightly, feeling the rough ironwork scratch his palms, and stared through the gates to the rows of gravestones which jutted up between tufts of yellow grass.

The graveyard sloped away from the entrance, graves marching down the hillside. At the rear of the cemetery a stone wall held back oak trees whose branches dipped over the wall's capstones and reached down into the graveyard. The branches swayed back and forth in the wind. When the branches moved, they revealed dark shadows. The silhouettes of the dead.

They came out from the shadows and drifted between the graves like mist rising from the lower end of the cemetery. Some were almost whole; fresh meat with just a blemish on their skin, others were barely walking. A woman in a long black dress was missing most of her face and the surface of her skull was stained peat-brown. A young man in a black T-shirt staggered against a headstone and when he put his hand out to steady himself Nick heard the distinctive sound of bone scraping against marble.

Hunger rolled from them in thick waves. Each breath Nick took dragged their stench into his lungs. He could taste their decay on his tongue; salty and dark like burned treacle.

They gathered on the other side of the cemetery fence and although they were a crowd, Nick was struck by the observation that each person was apart from the others. No one touched. Each person, perfectly alone.

The dead man stepped through the crowd and was immediately hidden from view. The urge to plunge through the gates and continue his argument was almost overwhelming, but instead Nick remained outside the iron railings.

A young boy stumbled forward. He reached the ornate gateway and passed onto the apron of cobblestones outside. Green moss furred the boy's cheeks. His eyes were sunken holes, black-rimmed and scarred. He held out his hand and his fingers were thin bones wrapped in decayed skin. The boy lunged forward, and Nick backed away.

The boy seemed to pause for a moment, deciding on whether to pursue Nick. He grinned and then staggered off in the opposite direction, heading down the hill toward the city centre. Looking to feed.

Nick considered rushing after him. He thought of the woman and her child. He thought of Abby. How many more people were going to die? He peered through the railings. The dead had already begun to dissipate, to slouch back into the depths of the cemetery. After just a few minutes Nick stared onto an empty graveyard.

Everyone assumed the fence was there as a boundary to protect the dead from the living. A combination of Victorian body snatchers and latter-day vandals. He knew the fence was there to protect the living from the dead. In his dreams he came to this place with fire and burned away the sickness. He came seeking vengeance and justice. He was filled with a desperate need to stop them preying on the living.

In his dreams he was a hero.

In reality, he stood outside the gates, too afraid even to enter the graveyard. The fear burned through him and although he tried to bully himself into passing through the gateway, the prospect of protecting Abby was not enough to get him to move.

After half an hour standing outside the cemetery, he gave up. He turned away, not daring to look back in case he witnessed the dead returning from their hiding places to watch him retreat.

CHAPTER 5

At the bottom of the hill Nick pulled his mobile phone from his pocket and called Abby's number. The phone rang against his ear twice before switching to her answer phone. He tried the number again, and this time the recorded voice immediately asked him to leave a message.

"I'm sorry. It was stupid to have... Just stupid." He paused to think if he could add anything else but hung up with most of what he needed to tell her left unsaid.

He drifted back into town and stood in the Market Square, inspecting the faces of people as they passed. He tried Abby's phone again but still received no reply. He hadn't expected her to wait, and yet he still felt a pang of irritation at her absence.

He walked across the square, returning to the mouth of the alley where the dead men had hunted. He glanced around as if he might find a secret trapdoor to explain their arrival. There was nothing, of course. They had shambled down from the cemetery like lost rats and, after feeding, they had made their way back home.

The thought chilled him. That thing had fed on Abby.

His phone chirruped and he checked the screen. *Where are you?*

He thumbed a quick response. *I'm in the Market Square. Where do you want to meet up?*

Costa. You're buying.

He stuffed the phone into his pocket and started walking. He moved with his shoulders curved and his head bowed down to the floor.

A ragged man in a dirty brown coat sat outside Tesco with a coffee cup in front of him. Nick resisted the temptation to kick the cup away and send the few coins scattering into the gutter. He tried not to look at the man too closely; he was not one of *them*, he was homeless, but Nick didn't dare to take the risk.

He brushed past a couple of teenagers and muttered an apology. As he got closer to the café he thought about Abby. His mind played with images. He imagined Abby, her hair thick with mud from her own grave and her skin as grey as a November sky. Rotting flesh hanging from her bones. Her cheekbones rising up through her face, skin pulled tight over them. He wondered: *If she comes back, will she try and find me?*

She stood outside the café, arms crossed. As Nick approached, she looked up and a flicker of annoyance crossed her face but when he reached her she opened her arms. His step stuttered. Quickly he checked her face; her hands; her wrists. There was no sign the infection had progressed. Yet. He moved forward. Abby opened her arms and he stepped backwards.

"Why did you take off?"

"Americano?" he asked. He stepped into the café and was greeted by the low rumble of conversations and the hiss of the coffee machine. He joined the short queue and concentrated on the neck of the man in front.

"Nick...?"

"It's complicated."

He didn't turn to look at her. He focussed on the kid with the paper cap over her hair who was making the coffees. She emerged from a cloud of steam, like some great magician.

When his turn came, the Barista placed two cups on a plastic tray and Nick headed for a table at the back of the café.

"Where did you go?" Abby asked when they sat down.

Nick looked up from his drink. The coffee stained her lips but beneath that he was sure they had returned to their natural colour. He took a deep breath but when he exhaled there were no words there.

"What's wrong?"

Nick looked to her neck where the dead man had touched her, but there was no sign of the black marks. Maybe he had just imagined them. Maybe the contact had not been enough to infect her. He fixed his eyes on a spot just over her shoulder.

"Why won't you look at me?" she asked, but Nick continued to focus on a poster at the front of the café.

"My mother died when I was a kid." He dared to steal a glance at Abby and the only emotion on her face was confusion.

Abby reached out to place her hand on top of his and Nick jerked his hand away. *Maybe she isn't infectious.* But he looked again for a sign the rot had begun to settle into her bones.

"I'm sorry."

Nick shrugged. "It was a long time ago."

"Your dad brought you up?" Abby asked.

"He doesn't matter," Nick said. Too quickly – he realised it as soon as he spoke. "It's not important." It was true. Almost.

He watched Abby's face as she decided to let it go and pick up with him another time. "Your mum died..." she prompted.

Nick nodded his head but said nothing, trying to frame the words before he said anything aloud. It was like navigating a maze – working out how to get from here to there. Only his destination was somewhere he didn't want to go, and Abby couldn't recognise that.

"I was fourteen."

"That's tough."

"They killed her."

He watched the shock hit Abby. It widened her eyes until they were so large it felt like she could see everything. Her eyebrows lifted in a comical expression. He watched her struggle for what to say and he knew it was impossible. She couldn't ask the right questions. Not in a million years.

She spoke slowly. Tentatively. Feeling her way through the conversation. He'd said to her that she should be a teacher or a counsellor – she was wasted in that insurance place.

"Who were they?" she asked.

The dead. He tried to say it aloud, but his lips refused to form the words. Abby sat waiting for an answer – she deserved at least that much – and he felt the words trapped in his throat.

She reached out her hand and he knew she was trying to comfort him, but all he wanted to do was scream at her to stop trying to touch him.

"Mum was ill for a long time before she died." He heard the words spilling from his mouth and knew he made no sense. In his head he was eloquent as he explained exactly who the dead were and how they had stolen the life from his mum and how the man in the courtyard had now done the same to Abby.

"He touched you."

"Who?"

"The man in the alley."

Abby shrugged. No big deal. She'd forgotten him already. The homeless were everywhere; they could be found begging outside of Tesco's or sitting on the street corner beside the ATM to guilt people into giving them a little loose change. Following people through the alley and clawing them until they gave some money was just another tactic. He could see what she was thinking, and he wanted to tell her she was wrong.

He stared at the skin which covered the delicate bones of her wrist. He saw fine blonde hairs and tiny freckles and the pale brown tan from the summer sun. There was nothing to suggest illness.

"I overreacted," he said. As soon as he spoke the lie, he felt the tension slip away. It was easy to reconcile himself to it – she didn't need to know. Not yet. She couldn't do anything about it, and she wouldn't believe him if he told her. "Sorry."

Part of him wanted her to put aside the thoughtful, careful Abby and force him to tell her what had happened in the courtyard. She needed to know, but instead she backed away from the conversation.

She couldn't make the connection between the homeless man in the courtyard and the death of his mother. He didn't give her enough information to join the dots and he wondered what she was thinking. That his mum had been killed by some homeless guy? A mugging gone wrong? It felt cruel not to explain it to her, but he looked down at her hand. Her long, perfect fingers.

He took a sip of coffee. It was cold. "London then? Are you looking forward to it?" There was a moment of indecision in her eyes, a moment when she might press him on what was going on, and then he saw it pass. Her smile was weak, tentative, but it started at the edge of her lips and finally made it to her eyes.

"I suppose so," she said.

Chapter 6

It was late when Nick got home. He paused in the car park at the foot of his block of flats, and looked up. His room was on the fifth floor and from the ground it was impossible to pick out his own window. He stood next to a smattering of broken glass from one of the cars. The person in the car park was different to the Nick Teel who had walked out of his flat that morning. Since his dad had left, everything had felt impersonal, as if the dead were nothing to do with him. Now that had changed.

The lights in the foyer poured onto the hard concrete and flashed off every cube of glass. It was supposed to make him feel safe. Rather than wait for the lift he opted for the stairs and some part of him understood that forcing his tired muscles up the five flights of steps was a self-inflicted punishment. It didn't make any difference to Abby, she would never even know, and when he reached the fifth floor with sweat dripping down his back and his calve muscles aching, he didn't feel his penance was complete.

The living room was cold. He walked across to the window and opened the curtains. The cityscape was lit in gaudy patches of yellow and white. The parks and the offices and the factories wallowed in pools of darkness between the streetlamps.

Once, he and Abby tried to get onto the roof and take in all of the city in a graceful 360° sweep. The door had been locked with a thick chain looped around the emergency escape push-bar. Instead, they had stood on the staircase, arms linked together, pointing out the Girls' School and the patch of scrubland where a row of terraced houses had been demolished; the square block of the old lace factories, the open sweep of the cemetery. Nick remembered that he had seen figures moving amongst the tombstones.

The memory felt tainted. It reminded him of what he had lost. No, not what he had lost - what they had stolen from him.

I played by the rules, he thought to himself. *And this is what I get in return?*

He unlocked the glass doors and stepped onto the small balcony. The wind snagged at his clothing. He wrapped his hands around the balustrade, feeling the cold steel edges press against his skin.

He wasn't going to let the dead man take Abby.

He heard a sound. The soft, slurred sound of a dragged footstep. For a moment he thought they were in the room behind him. Fear flushed through him. He stood, gripping the railing tightly and listening to the dead as they shuffled past. It was too quiet, too subtle. It was not in the room, not even on the fifth floor of the tower block. It was somewhere further away, as if the dead wanted to remind him that they were still there.

He listened to the sound as it faded, and only when it was gone, did he allow himself to breathe once more.

CHAPTER 7

Nick waited for the first five digits of the phone number to register before cancelling the call. He stared at the mobile cradled in the palm of his hand. The screen recorded each failed attempt he had made to call his father. Seven times in the past hour.

He sat on the floor, curled into a foetal position between the wall and the bed. Part of him recognised that he had regressed to childhood. Maybe in time he would crawl under his bed and seek refuge in the shadows and the dust.

In his head, he ran through an opening line once more before he pressed the number on the screen. Through the tinny speaker he heard the numbers dial and then the distant sound of a phone ringing.

His dad picked up on the third ring, as if he had been sitting there waiting for the last hour and only now decided to answer.

"Hello?"

"Dad." All the words he had crafted were lost. Nick listened to his father's thick breathing.

The wind battered at the balcony doors. It whistled through a gap in the brickwork. Nick imagined he could hear the same wind whispering to him through the phone's speaker.

When there was no instant reply Nick chose to keep talking. "Dad, I need your help. The..."

The line went dead. The scratchy background noise of the call was replaced by a high-pitched electronic whine.

"Bastard," Nick muttered. He pressed his thumb hard against the glass screen of his phone.

You're going to talk to me, Nick thought as he waited for the phone to connect again. The phone began to ring and stopped immediately.

Nick dialled again, and when his father cut the line, he tried again. This time the number was busy. He threw his phone onto the bed. "You can't do that. It's not right."

He had his father's address. Didn't the old man realise that? Didn't he understand that if he refused to answer the phone Nick could go down there and seek him out? It would take a couple of hours to get to Bristol, but he would do it out of sheer spite now, just to prove to his father that he couldn't abandon him.

Nick crawled onto the bed and tried to think of someone else he could call. It took him a moment to accept that there was no one. No one from work who would understand. No brothers or sisters or aunts or uncles. His father had made sure there was just the two of them.

He got up to draw the curtains. When he returned to his bed, he closed his eyes and all he could see were images of Abby. Abby standing at the side of the pavement. Abby following him when he had told her to wait. Abby when the dead man brushed his fingers against her shoulder.

He thought about walking across town just to lie beside her. To be close to her. His apartment felt empty, as if he was not even present, and against that the risk she might infect him seemed almost worth taking.

Almost.

Under the covers, still fully dressed, he shivered at the image of the man in the courtyard with his broken skin and sunken eyes. Infested and infected. He left the phone where it was and closed his eyes and tried to sleep, tried to push away the images of the day that crawled into his mind.

CHAPTER 8

An hour later the phone rang.

Nick woke from a light sleep. He'd been dreaming about... something, but as soon as he tried to grasp the images they melted away.

He grabbed for the phone, his hand clattering against the side of the night table before he made contact. The light from the screen flashed against the ceiling.

"Hello," Nick said. His voice slurred. His tongue felt heavy.

"What do you want?"

The last vestiges of sleep washed from his mind as he recognised the voice.

"Dad."

His mind stopped. What *did* he want? He took a breath and was immediately worried he had taken too long to respond. It was dark outside, proper night. Nick peered through the window and wondered what the view was like where his dad was sitting.

"I need help," he said. The response felt wrong. *Help* was an understatement. "I need a miracle."

His dad laughed. A short, harsh bark. "I can't help you with that."

"It's about *them*."

"Of course, it is."

Nick bit down on the urge to apologise again. He tried to imagine what his father was doing. How he was feeling. His sentences were short. His words were tightly bound.

"There were so many times when I wanted to call you, but I didn't know what to say." Nick recognised was talking too fast. There was only silence in response to his words.

"They've claimed someone," Nick said. He took a breath. Saying it aloud felt like a confession.

"And?"

The room swirled around Nick. And? *And?* He'd just explained what had happened to Abby. What else was there to say?

"I need to stop them."

"You can't."

"I *have* to."

"There is nothing you can do. Nothing." The anger in his father's voice brought back memories of sitting in his bedroom and listening to his parents downstairs, their voices ringing off the walls. *I'd forgotten*, Nick realised. *Or chose to forget*, he thought to himself.

"This woman – it is a woman, isn't it?" his father asked. He continued speaking without waiting for an answer. "There's nothing you can do to help her now. Don't you think I would have done it when they took your mother?"

No, Nick wanted to say. *You gave up too easily*. But he held his silence. He visualised a gossamer thread; thin and fragile. With the wrong word the connection between them would break.

"There must be something."

"Don't you think I tried?"

The pain in his father's words was frightening. Nick wasn't sure why, but he hadn't expected that. Not from the man who had stood in the kitchen and screamed into his face to get out. Nick understood he held that image of his father in his mind – his cheeks ruddy, his eyes blazing and his hands pulled into tight fists. *That* was his dad. Small and hard and invulnerable. He didn't recognise the man on the other end of the phone.

He spoke slowly, the weight of each syllable perfectly measured. "There has to be something."

"She's infected?"

"Only a few hours. She doesn't even know."

"It doesn't matter. They've claimed her. It's over."

"What if they take someone else?"

"They won't. You know that. They feed until their claim is exhausted, and *then* they find someone new."

"There has to be something."

"I tried everything to save your mother."

"No." Nick spoke before he had a chance to think about what he was saying. "No, you didn't. Because you failed."

The line went dead.

Nothing less than saving her would have been enough. That was why they couldn't be together. That was why even living in the same country seemed too close.

CHAPTER 9

Nick sat in Abby's kitchen and watched as she bustled between the counter and the hob. There was nothing in the way she moved to suggest she was ill. The kitchen had the same nuclear-war appearance she always managed to achieve whenever she cooked even the simplest meal, and as she prepared the pasta, she was telling him about a client at work who had come into the office for a meeting.

She wore a grey sweatshirt that came up to her chin, so it wasn't possible to see where the man had touched her the previous day. Nick peered closely at the skin around her throat but there was no sign the infection had spread.

It took him a moment to realise she had stopped talking. The silence in the kitchen settled like snow and he wondered how long she had been standing there looking at him before he'd noticed.

"What's wrong?" Abby asked.

Her voice sounded normal. No slurring. No indication that she was struggling to keep up with what was happening around her. He didn't know how the infection would surface; with his mother it had been a painfully slow progression that had eaten away at her for nearly a year. If that happened to Abby, then she might not show any symptoms for months.

"What do you mean?"

He knew as soon as he spoke that he had been too slow to respond.

"You keep staring at me..."

"Can't I take a moment to appreciate your beauty?"

She pressed her lips together in a thin line; an expression she only ever made when she was angry. *At me?* Nick tried to work out what he might have done to upset her. He'd only been in the house ten minutes and all of that time had been spent listening to her talk about her day at work. He hadn't had an opportunity to upset her.

"Don't," she said.

"Don't want?"

"Pretend."

He nearly asked her then: *How much do you know?* There was a feeling of relief that he didn't have to hide it from her anymore. Maybe as soon as the man had touched her, she'd realised he had passed something onto her.

Nick felt the muscles in his shoulders relax. If she already knew then it made everything so much easier.

"Every time I come near you, you flinch."

The water in the pan boiled over and sizzled against the blue flame. Abby took a second to adjust the heat but she didn't take her eyes off Nick, as if she was afraid he would slip away.

He shrugged. The gesture felt impotent.

"Tell me," she said. "Whatever it is, I deserve to know the truth."

He looked into her eyes and tried to decide if the hazel colour was stained with the first traces of milky-white. He pushed away the thought of what it would be like to watch her fading away. At the end his mother had been angry; lying in bed and criticising anyone who came near her. She'd blamed her husband for her illness. Would Abby be like that? He would have thought it impossible and yet the way she had snapped at him betrayed a hint of what to expect when the illness took hold.

"I... I..." he started to say.

She was holding a wooden spoon in her right hand as if she was deciding whether to club him with it. A wisp of hair freed itself from her brow and fell in front of her face. He wanted to laugh, and he wanted her to laugh with him, but he wasn't sure how she would react, so he kept silent.

"Who is she?"

"What?"

"I'm not going to pretend I'm not angry or hurt, but lying about it just makes it worse."

Nick started to rise from the chair, his arms outstretched to gather her in. "Do you think I'm having an affair?"

"Aren't you?"

"No," he said. The relief stained his voice and now he did laugh. "Why would you ever think that?" He took a step forward and understood if he moved any closer he would have to embrace her. There was no sign of any stain on her neck. He checked her wrists where they emerged from the cuffs of the sweatshirt.

"Stop it!" she shouted at him.

I can't.

He stood there for a moment, his arms outstretched but unable to touch her. He wanted to move forward and embrace her, but he couldn't.

He dropped his hands to his side. "He touched you."

"Who?" Abby looked confused. Suspicious. As if she thought this was a ploy to distract her from her accusations.

"The man in the alley."

"What has he got to do with the way you're behaving?"

Nick swallowed. This wasn't how he had imagined it would happen. He had never told anyone before. It had been the secret he shared only with his dad. Even as his mother lay dying, the cause was a shadow at the edge of their conversations. He thought that when he did finally tell someone it would be because it was the right time, not because they were already infected.

"He needed it to carry on living, but he'll keep coming back to take more. Until you fade away. That's what they do." He spoke without pause so that Abby would not have the opportunity to interrupt him. When he finished, he watched for her reaction, but there was nothing. He couldn't tell if it was disbelief or apathy.

It was a mistake; he understood that immediately. He pressed on. There was no alternative. "They die, and they need to feed off people to survive. It's what they did to mum. It's what he's doing to you. I don't know if there's anything we can do to stop it, but we have to try."

Abby turned her back and shook her head. He paused, trying to think of something that would make it better.

"Just go," Abby said.

"I'm sorry," Nick said.

She was crying. She tried to pretend otherwise, but he could tell from the way her shoulders bowed inward. He went to her, placed a hand squarely in the centre of her shoulders, away from any skin, any infection. She shrugged off his touch but said nothing and after a moment Nick let himself out

The curtains of the house opposite shivered as he stepped onto the path. He saw the outline of a figure against the light of the room beyond. *The Neighbourhood Witch*. Abby had warned him about her – a woman who spent every free moment staring out of her window. He considered shouting something at her: *Seen enough?* But she wasn't the problem – he was.

CHAPTER 10

He dumped his jacket over the back of the sofa and went to get a drink. He didn't turn on the lights, so the bottles and kitchen appliances looked like dark ghosts. He opened the fridge and cool light washed over him. There were a few bottles of lager, but he wanted something that would burn. Something that would convince him he was still alive. He closed the fridge and reached into one of the cupboards to retrieve a bottle of Bushmills. He couldn't even remember why he had the whiskey – it must have been a gift from someone.

He returned to the sofa with the bottle and a glass and poured himself a measure before stretching out and staring at the ceiling. The first drink scorched his throat, just as he wanted. He coughed as it went down, and rubbed tears away from his eyes.

"It's not my fault," he said to the empty room. "It's not *just* my fault." He had to accept some of the blame, but there was more than enough to go around. It was the dead – greedy bastards who had to leech off others once their time was up. It was his father – for isolating him and then abandoning him. It was Abby – for not allowing herself to believe and needing answers he couldn't give. But, yes, it was his fault too. He wanted to be someone else – someone who would take Abby into his arms and damn the consequences. Someone who could persuade her that she was in danger. That wasn't him. He was too weak. Too feeble. He took another slug of whiskey.

A different Nick Teel wouldn't have accepted all the years of watching the dead prey upon the living. He was just doing what his father had taught him in order to survive, but what good was that when he was alone?

He poured another measure into the glass and held it to his lips and then thought, *work tomorrow*. He paused, and then drank the whiskey down anyway. To hell with them. To hell with Mark Hanscomb and all the rest of them. The office was a prison. He hated it. Hated it.

He picked up the phone and dialled his work number from memory. The voicemail kicked in and a woman's voice – Sally? Hannah? – told him the office was closed and asked him to call back during opening hours. He considered leaving a message but it wasn't even the possibility that they would recognise his voice that stopped him. He had nothing to say to them.

He tried his father next. Somewhere down in Bristol the phone rang and rang and eventually tripped over to voicemail and encouraged him to leave a message. "It's me. You know, your son. The one you left behind. The one who didn't die."

And then he rang Abby.

He expected the call to go to voicemail, but instead she picked up immediately.

"I'm sorry," he said.

"What's wrong with you?"

He shrugged, and then realised she wouldn't be able to see the gesture. The line popped and cracked with static and in that moment she seemed a long way from him. A distance measured not just by miles. He wondered if that gap was permanent.

"I love you," he said.

She hesitated before replying. "I know." But he wasn't sure that was the truth. He didn't trust himself to recognise the truth anymore.

He listened to Abby breathing down the line. There was more he should say but he couldn't, not like this. After a few minutes Abby said softly "I'm going to hang up now," and then the pop and crackle of the open line was replaced with the whine of the broken connection.

He put the phone down on the floor next to the bottle. The right thing now would be to drag himself to bed. Instead, he lay on the sofa and let a ragged, ugly sleep creep over him.

CHAPTER 11

It was a lie. Every breath in, every breath out. Everything he did. Everything he thought. Everything he said. All of it was a lie.

Nick stared through the computer screen and his mind fogged with the disconnect between what he was doing and what was actually important. He sat there, pecking at the keyboard. Abby was infected and still he sat at his desk like a good boy and answered the phone and typed out orders like nothing was wrong. He wanted to blame his father, but the excuse was hollow. Nick's memories were blurred by fear and grief, but at least his dad hadn't simply turned out for work each day and waited for his wife to die.

Abby's not going to die, Nick thought to himself.

He slammed down the phone and from the corner of his eye he noticed Mark look up from his desk.

He loosened his tie because it felt more like a noose than a piece of clothing. Nick looked around the office at his colleagues in their identikit clothing – a uniform in everything but name – and he hated them. But more than them, he hated himself. They didn't know any better. They didn't hear the footsteps of the dead walking across the concrete slabs of the Market Square. They didn't catch the wet stink of rotting flesh. They didn't close their eyes and see a man stumbling forward to steal a woman's life.

He pushed his chair back from the desk and headed for the door. He needed air. He needed to be away from that tight room where everyone peered into their computer screens with an intensity that suggested what they were doing was important.

"Nicholas?" Mark called to him, but the summons was easy to ignore. Nick slammed the door open with the heel of his hand and clattered down the back stairs. He let himself out through the emergency exit. As soon as the door opened the silence of the stairwell was shattered. A lorry blasted past. A man shouted across the street.

Nick stood with his back against the rough stone of the building and closed his eyes. He needed a cigarette. He didn't smoke, and yet the urge to stand there and draw in a lungful of nicotine was almost overwhelming. A cigarette and nothing to worry about for just five minutes.

The pavement trembled beneath him as a bus pulled away from the kerb, leaving behind a line of people. The voice of a newspaper hawker drifted over to him. Nick smiled at a childhood memory of the woman who had stood on the corner of the Market Square each evening as he came home from school, calling out 'Post. Evening Post,' in a public school voice. She was gone now, he didn't know where or why, and *The Evening Post* had been replaced by *The Post* as it gradually crept out earlier and earlier to compete with the national dailies.

Before he even heard the headline the newspaper hawker was calling, Nick recognised something was wrong. He leaned into the wind, as if he needed the extra few inches to better hear the man.

Nick started to walk toward the small, yellow cabin. All he could see was the back wall plastered with newsbills proclaiming '729 jobs in today's Post' and 'Full Match report'. There was a small plastic window at the back of the box and the first sight Nick caught of the hawker was the back of his head – grey hair thinning over a grey scalp.

He had reached the front of the box when the newspaper hawker shouted out his headline again: "Tragedy as daughter dies in the night."

A wave of nausea swept over Nick and his vision shifted from full colour to monochrome. He tasted dirt at the back of his mouth. Grave dirt. *They're com-*

ing, he thought and started to look around, but after a moment he understood his mind was simply freewheeling in panic.

The newspaper seller was in his late fifties. He held out a rolled-up newspaper in one hand and the other was outstretched for payment. Nick pressed a pound into the man's hand and snatched the paper. He didn't wait for change, but instead hurried away with the newspaper pressed to his chest.

He only dared to unfold the newspaper when he was safely tucked into a corner. He squatted down, knees jutting out before him, his head at waist height to the stream of people who passed by him.

The front page of *The Post* was dominated by a photograph of a woman and her child. Even as he recognised them, he desperately hoped it was someone else.

Her name was Jane Hamilton. The text below the photograph went on to report that she was seven and lived in a flat in Basford with her mother, Marjorie. Or had lived...

Nick put his hand out to steady himself. An image of Marjorie's daughter, lips and eyes ringed with blue, was instant and perfect. For a second it felt as if the whole world had slipped from its axis, just enough to pitch him off balance.

More information was offered on page five, but Nick didn't have the strength to open the paper. He tried to stand. The ground below him shifted and the only way he was able to retain his balance was by walking his hands up the wall until he stood with his forehead pressed against the rough brick as he waited for wave after wave of horror to pass.

Too soon. It's too soon.

He was aware that the people gathered around the bus stop were staring at him. *Let them look*, he thought. What people thought of him wasn't important. They didn't understand. None of them did.

He sucked in a heavy breath of air and the familiar taste of cigarette smoke and petrol fumes was almost welcome. He searched around for something to focus on. Something to stop his mind fracturing into a thousand panicked thoughts.

The clock must have been a remnant from an earlier building on the site; an ornate Victorian piece with gold and blue edgings bolted to the side of a concrete office block. Salvaging it had probably been a sop to the heritage brigade. Maybe it had originally been beautiful, in context, but now it just looked ugly. Better for everyone if it had been torn down with the rest of the old building. Nick stared at the object until his panic subsided.

When Nick looked down at his hands, they had stopped shaking. He could still feel the pressure crowding his mind, threatening to break through. *She's gone already?* He thought. He felt the panic starting to rise again and had to work hard to push it away.

They had taken the girl after just one day. Had Jane Hamilton known what was happening to her?

He could see the grinning face of the dead man as he touched Abby's neck.

Nick dialled Abby's number and started to walk, taking long strides with legs that felt weak and fragile. He walked with his head bent down, staring at the ground. He bumped into people as he hurried toward his destination. All he cared about was the sound of Abby's ringing phone as he willed her to answer.

He stepped out in front of a car and woke from his fugue when the driver blasted the horn. Nick looked through the windscreen at the driver who wore an expression of weary rage – as if she was used to stupid pedestrians stepping out in front of her. Nick shrugged his shoulders and retreated to the pavement.

"Answer the phone," he muttered into the speaker. The call went to voicemail and before the voice had a chance to encourage him to leave a message he hung up and redialled. He imagined Abby sitting in her office with the phone ringing while she was in a meeting.

He thought about the pattern of black marks on Abby's skin and imagined the dead man stumbling through the corridor toward her office. Trying different rooms until he came upon Abby.

The phone went to voicemail a second time. Nick hung up and redialled.

The shortest route to Abby's office was across the Market Square, but as Nick approached, he knew he was afraid. Instead, he took the road around the back of the buildings so he wouldn't have to see the slab of open ground. It wasn't logical. Just because the dead had fed in the square last time, didn't have any bearing on where they would choose next. He had seen them walking through the Victoria Shopping Centre and the train station. He had seen them at a Nottingham Forest football match. They hunted wherever they could find people. But still, he turned his back on the square and stumbled along the pavement, holding the phone to his ear and praying Abby would answer.

He reached the corner.

The stench of dead flesh was subtle, almost sweet. He smelled it for a moment before it registered in his thoughts.

The man had his back to him, but Nick didn't need to see the man's face to know he was one of them.

He turned around – a pleasant looking man, his nose slightly bent as if he had taken a good punch in his youth. His eyes were bloodshot – too much time spent out on the beer. When he grinned, there was a gap where one of his teeth was missing. His skin had the too-bright colour of one who had fed recently.

The first traces of milky-white tainted the man's eyes and Nick wondered how well the man could see.

"How long does it last?" Nick asked. "A month? A week? A day? How long before you're just a husk of rotting flesh again?"

The man stared at Nick as if they spoke different languages. His eyelids closed over those milky-white eyes and hid them.

"Was it worth killing someone for your few extra days?" Nick asked. He stepped forward and he could smell the stench of the dead man's breath. It sang of blow flies and maggots and meat liquefying in a hot room. He tried to hold his breath against the stench, but it was already inside him. It clung to his skin, his clothes. It was in his nostrils and his throat and his stomach. Nick coughed and tasted the dead man's scent on his lips.

Before yesterday they had always been strangers seen across a crowded street. Before, he had run away when he had come across them. They were not his problem.

Nick lunged forward, his hands outstretched, ready to seize the man by the throat. He stopped just before he made contact, his hands hanging in the air. The man did not flinch.

"You don't think I'll do it, do you?" Nick said. "Because if I touch you..."

He paused. If the man's prey was still alive then he would be safe, but if that last feed had taken them then he was lethal. How was anyone to know? The man grinned as if he understood the dilemma perfectly.

"You can't do this," Nick said. "I won't let you."

The dead man turned and walked away. Nick noticed flecks of white dandruff on his shoulders. The dead man stumbled – missed half a step – and when he continued, he moved with an almost imperceptible limp that Nick was certain was new.

He thought about following him and then... and then what? He'd already tried that. He let the dead man walk away because in truth he did not know what else to do.

Instead, he returned to his original mission. Abby's offices were just a few streets away. He bowed his head as he walked through the streets so that he wouldn't see another of the dead, and he walked into the foyer of Abby's building.

The lift dropped him outside the reception. If pressed, Nick would have to confess that he had only a vague understanding of Abby's job; something to do with insurance. At social gatherings her work colleagues would retreat to a jargon-filled language of annuities and superannuated interest and Quals. He asked her to sit down once and explain Quals to him – Quality of Life, a measurement they used to determine how much someone's life was worth.

£70,000 a year, apparently.

The boy at the desk grinned. "Welcome to Harwood Insurance. How can I help?"

"I'm here to see Abby."

"Is she expecting you?"

Nick hesitated. "No," he said eventually, drawing out the single word into a long sound. "She's not expecting me, but..."

"That's fine. I'll just give her a call to let her know you're here."

While the boy picked up the phone, Nick looked at the wall at the back of the reception. A framed certificate proclaimed Harwood as runners-up in last year's Insurance Industry awards for the creative annuities category.

Nick was aware the boy was talking, but after his initial cheery voice he had dropped to a lower tone.

The boy put down the phone and Nick immediately returned his attention to the youthful, round face.

"I'm sorry, Abby isn't available at present."

"I need to see her."

"Abby is with a client."

"I'll wait." Nick checked for a chair, but there was none. He shrugged his shoulders and looked back at the boy.

"The meeting is scheduled to last all afternoon."

"I'm fine," Nick said. He thought of the empty desk back at his own office and imagined Mark sitting there glaring at his chair. "I can wait," he said.

He could feel the boy's discomfort, and while he knew he had caused it, it wasn't enough to put him off his strategy. The boy shifted in his chair and glanced at the telephone. What was he planning to do?

"I have to see her," Nick said. "I just need to make sure that she's okay. You know how it is?" He looked at the boy, who looked like he should still be in school learning about integers and practising his joined-up writing rather than sitting there telling him that Abby was unavailable.

Nick thought about rushing past the boy. The kid looked all of nine stone and wouldn't be able to stop a charging dung beetle. But storming into Abby's office wouldn't help anyone. He could hardly stand there and tell her about the dead men and Jane Hamilton. She wouldn't believe him.

"Tell Abby I called," Nick said. "And tell her I'll come 'round tonight."

"I will," the boy said. He looked relieved, as if he had been expecting a confrontation, as if he thought Nick was the sort of man who might become physical in order to get what he wanted. It was written there in the boy's taut posture. *Where did that come from?* Nick wondered. He'd never been in a fight, not even in school. How did he give the impression he was ready to swing a punch?

Nick replayed his sentence and realised that to the wrong person it could sound like a threat. He wondered what the boy would say to Abby when she was finally rid of her client. If she had ever really been in a meeting.

He reached for the door and discovered he had to relax his hand from a tight fist before he was able to take hold of the handle.

He closed the door gently behind him, making sure it made no noise as it closed. Because he didn't slam doors, just like he didn't threaten people.

CHAPTER 12

When Nick returned to his office after a two-hour absence, Mark started to rise from his seat, but then thought otherwise.

For his part, Nick hunched in front of his computer. His whole body was knotted, each muscle pulled tight. He stared at the screen and typed without thinking, conscious only of the heavy sound of his fingers hitting the keys.

He abandoned the report he was supposed to be writing and dipped into his email. There were a couple of new requests for quotations, followed by an all-staff message reminding everyone that the database was going offline at 4.00 pm on Friday for maintenance.

He had to scroll down the page to find Abby's last email. Reading her words, it seemed impossible to believe they were written just a few days earlier. The email was about nothing in particular – just the end of a conversation that had bounced back and forth between them over the course of the day about whether to go and see a film.

Nick hit the reply button and sat with his hands poised above the keyboard. He typed an email and then read it back and deleted everything he had written. He tried again, and once more he deleted everything. It wasn't right; he was trying too hard.

He typed: "I need to see you," and pressed send before he had a chance to think about it any further. As soon as it was gone, he knew it wouldn't make any difference. He watched for a reply from her, and when none came immediately, he clicked *refresh*.

After five minutes the only email he received was a piece of spam inviting him to attend a training course to become a Finance Entrepreneur. He deleted the message and waited for Abby's reply.

He clicked *refresh*.

Mark drifted across the office towards Nick. He looked as if he was crossing into the sort of territory that might be marked on a map with the legend 'Here be Tygers'. Nick glared at him.

"That report. The one for Thursday."

The folder for the report was on the right-hand side of Nick's desk. He put his hand down on the cover, claiming it as his own.

"When do you think it will be ready?"

Nick toyed with the idea of pretending he didn't know what Mark was referring to. Instead, he picked up the folder and handed it over. "I've already finished it."

It was sickening to see the relief on Mark's face. As if the future of someone's life rested on whether Nick had been able to complete the assessment on time.

"It's not important," Nick said. "You know that, don't you?"

Mark tapped the folder with his hand. He pursed his lips and Nick was sure he wouldn't dare to say anything.

"Long lunch today."

"Yes," Nick agreed.

Mark nodded

"I didn't know where you were."

"I went out."

Nick wondered what would happen if he explained everything to Mark. His boss would finally realise that some things were more important than reports and lunch hours.

"It made it difficult to cover the lunch period. For the phones. Sally had to stay behind"

Nick glared. Mark wanted him to say sorry, but he was done with apologies. They didn't make any difference.

"If you could let me know next time you plan to stay out so long," Mark said.

Nick looked back down to his screen. He pressed *refresh*. Still no message from Abby. By the time he looked up, Mark had retreated to his desk clutching the all-important folder.

As soon as the Office Manager was gone, Mark sent a quick text to Abby, *Are you okay?* and put the handset under a sheaf of papers in case Mark came round again.

The pile of papers quivered, and he checked the screen. *I'm fine.*

I need to see you tonight.

Nick looked up from the keyboard. Mark was standing at the far end of the office, looking across the rows of desks like a general surveying his troops. He'd be happier if he could put them all on hamster wheels, spinning around for eight hours a day. Nick pushed his mobile to the side of the desk where he could keep an eye on it. He carried on typing and watching Mark from the corner of his eye as he patrolled the room. It took ten minutes for Abby to reply.

Not tonight.

He snatched the phone and thumbed a response. *I'm worried about you.*

The reply was almost instant, and he imagined Abby sitting in her office, walls covered with her certificates.

Not tonight.

He checked – Mark was standing beside Sally, deep in conversation. Nick snatched his phone. He reached the stairwell before calling Abby's number.

She answered immediately. "Give me some space, Nick."

"I..."

He needed to tell her about Jane. He needed to explain about the man in the alley and the grey marks on her shoulder. He wanted to tell her about his mum and how it had taken her a year to die, and how he couldn't speak to his dad anymore because... well, because he didn't try hard enough to stop what happened. He had so much to say and yet he stuttered over the first word and when he tried to breathe it was like someone had reached into his chest and squeezed all the air out of his lungs.

She hung up before he could think of a response.

He stood, looking at the blank screen of the phone. His thumbs hovered over the screen with Abby's number. He considered redialling, but what was the point? She'd made it clear she wasn't going to listen to him.

Standing in the stairwell, looking up at a pale lamp that oozed yellow light over the stone staircase, he called his dad. There was a green emergency exit sign plastered against the concrete wall. That's exactly what he needed right now: an emergency exit.

Nick left a message on the voicemail and immediately rang the number again. Still no response. He tried again. Left a third message. "I can do this all afternoon," Nick said. "I can keep ringing and ringing until you give up and speak to me."

He thought of Abby in her office, chatting on the phone to someone about their life assurance policy. She was just a glorified salesperson too, no different to him. He thought about the smudges, bright against her pale skin. *Would it hurt?*

He nearly called her again, but it would only make things worse. He stuffed the phone in his pocket and went back into the office to discover whether Mark had noticed he was missing.

Chapter 13

Nick joined the five o'clock rush out of the office. Lying on a dirty piece of cardboard in the doorway of the shop next door was a young man. Nick watched as Sally brushed past without appearing to notice the man was there. Others followed and the young man stared down at the floor, an empty cup from a Gregg's coffee crumpled on the pavement in front of him. He stank of sweat rather than decay, and Nick assumed he was homeless; just as invisible to the Sallys and Marks of the world as the dead.

He found a coin in his pocket and dropped it into the paper cup. The young man did not look up but bobbed his head in silent gratitude.

He imagined the scene outside Harwood Insurance: Abby surrounded by all her work colleagues. Maybe if he turned up, she would forgive him and they would link arms and walk down to the pub for a drink, but the tone of her texts suggested otherwise. Showing up at her office would just make things worse. Instead, he walked into town and waited outside the Post Office for the number 76 which would take him to Abby's house.

He spent the bus ride staring out of the window, spotting the homeless and the dead as they sat in doorways and shuffled along the pavements. Sometimes it was impossible to tell them apart. He saw a woman shuffling along the pavement, wrapped in layers of tatty clothes. Dead? Homeless?

They hide in plain sight, Nick thought. He wondered how many were in the city, and if any other people knew they existed. He yearned for that ignorance – for the ability to look straight through the woman on the pavement.

The bus dropped him on the edge of Abby's estate, and he walked the familiar route to her house. He approached slowly, wary now he was there. There were no lights on in the house, but her car was parked by the kerb.

Nick glanced around the street – there was no sign of the dead man. Maybe he had taken enough from her to last a few weeks. But Nick felt he was clinging desperately to the idea. The man would come back to feed again. The only question was when.

For now, the street was empty. The only movement was the net curtains in the house opposite. He glared at the windows and the woman hidden behind them, and then returned to the task of protecting Abby.

His fingertips brushed the metal key in his pocket. He *could* let himself in. Instead, Nick peered through the downstairs windows of the house. It was strange looking in on the familiar rooms. He spied the sofa where they curled up to watch Abby's large-screen TV. The remains of her breakfast were still on a plate on the coffee table.

She could be lying on the bathroom floor, unable to call for help. She could have fallen into a coma. She could…

"Abby!" he shouted. "Abby, are you okay?" He put his ear to the door. There were no sounds from inside. At this point in a TV show he would kick down the door and burst into the house, searching each room until he found Abby lying semi-conscious. He would scoop her into his arms and walk back through the splintered remains of the front door as the hero.

Nick looked at the door. *Yeah, right.* The only thing that would happen if he tried to smash down the door would be a broken ankle and the Neighbourhood Witch calling the police.

He looked through the window to the right of the door. The room beyond was empty. He opened the letterbox and gagged as a stench flooded out.

Nick released the letterbox and straightened his back. He put his hand flat against the front door, as if testing for heat.

He stepped back from the doorstep. Upstairs the curtains were pulled tight and there was no sign of movement. He took the key from his pocket and paused. There was a sound from the rear of the house. He pictured Abby in the back garden, the dead man already at the house and feeding from her.

He hurried down the side of the house and let himself through a gate. Tall fence panels enclosed an untidy lawn. A washing line stretched from the corner of the house to a tree at the far end of the garden. There were two rows of concrete slabs between the lawn and the back of the house, and steps leading up to the back door.

The smell was even stronger here. Nick could taste it at the back of his throat: the thick, cloying soil and the rancid feel of wet meat.

The garden was empty, and yet he pressed his back against the kitchen door and his eyes flicked across the scene.

From the other side of the garden fence, he heard the sound again. The dead man murmured. There were words buried within the sound. Nick thought that if he listened hard enough, he would be able to determine what the man was saying.

The thing to do now was run away. It was a policy he'd followed all his life. It had kept him safe through the madness.

In the next garden, birds took to the wing. They hung in the air, drawn against the grey sky.

The wooden fence panels rocked against the concrete posts and the noise made Nick think of a closed fist knocking on the lid of a coffin.

Two hands grasped the top of the fence, fingers clawing against the wood. The dead man started to pull himself up.

CHAPTER 14

Nick held a scream trapped within his throat. The panel made a series of deep thunks as it hit the concrete fence posts.

He turned to hammer his fists against the door. "Abby! Let me in."

Behind him the fence panel rattled. Nick turned to check. The dead man was halfway over the fence. Clothes hung in tattered rags around his body. Even across the distance it was easy for Nick to see the grey skin and the rotten features of the man. Decay had stolen his nose. There was a hole on one side of his head instead of an eye socket, as if death was eating his insides.

Nick fled from the kitchen door. He stepped onto the stone patio and glanced around for a weapon. There was an overturned flowerpot; a pair of rusted secateurs; a pile of stones. He took a second glance at the secateurs and shuddered at the thought of slipping the steel jaws around the dead man's fingers and forcing them closed. Nick snatched a couple of stones and threw them. They clanged against the fence, not even close enough to cause the dead man to flinch. Nick picked up another stone and moved closer, walking onto the feral lawn.

His next stone struck the dead man in the face. The man glared at Nick but kept climbing. Through the ripped sleeves of his shirt Nick could see his arms straining to hoist the weight of his body over the fence panel. In places Nick saw the red cords of muscle. He swung over a leg. His shoe was covered in thick mud that tracked up his trouser leg almost to his knee, as if he had walked through a field to reach Abby's garden.

Nick rushed back and grabbed a handful of stones and threw them as he approached the fence. Even when the man was hit in the face the attack did not slow him. The wounds shone fresh and red and then faded amongst all the other cuts on his body.

The man shuddered as he hoisted his hips over the fence. He was perfectly balanced on top of the fence and Nick considered rushing forward and pushing him away. Instead, he held his position in the centre of the lawn and a moment later the dead man landed in a heap amongst Abby's flower beds.

Now I should run, Nick thought. *I've done my best, but now I should run.*

The thought rattled inside his mind but didn't make it to his limbs. He stood steadfast on the lawn.

"Leave her alone," he screamed.

The man moved slowly, dragging himself upright. His left arm hung limp against his side. There were fresh grazes on his face.

The man was no more than fifteen feet away. Downwind, Nick could smell the stink of his gums rotting inside his mouth.

"Keep away from me," Nick warned. The dead man twitched his head and groaned; a low noise that sounded like the stone lid of a sarcophagus being pushed aside. The sound passed through Nick, and he felt his knees buckle. The muscles in his legs became loose strings and all his attention was focussed on remaining upright.

The dead man took a crooked step forward and Nick heard the bones inside his body rub together, the cartilage rotted away to nothing.

"Stand up," Nick muttered to himself. His vision took on a grey hue; the colour washed from his sight. It had the effect of making the scene less realistic, as if he was looking at a monochrome photograph.

He heard a sound behind him.

Nick turned.

The door to the house was open.

It took a moment for his mind to process the information. There was a shape standing on the top step.

In his mind he was quick and yet in reality he lumbered across the lawn toward the door, staggering over divots with the grace of one of the undead. Behind him the man creaked and thumped and thudded his way across the grass.

Abby stood in the doorway.

Nick stopped.

She was dressed in blue jeans and a black T-shirt. Her clothes hung from her body, as if she had shed half her bodyweight. Her eyes were rimmed with brown circles.

He stopped. The dead man did not.

CHAPTER 15

Nick turned his head slightly to find the dead man behind him. The distance between them was no more than a half-dozen feet; not quite enough for the man to reach out and claim him.

Abby's body was locked tight with shock. She stood in the doorway.

"Who is that?" she asked. Nick pushed his way into the house and slammed the door behind him. He turned the key in the lock and pushed home the bolts at the top and bottom of the door.

Abby turned to Nick. "What have you done?"

He opened his mouth, trying to frame a response. The dead man slammed his body against the door. Both Nick and Abby jumped in surprise.

"What is he doing in my garden?"

"I'm sorry," Nick said. *Where to start?* He thought.

"Why is he here?"

"It's complicated."

"Well, uncomplicate it."

The man banged again on the back door. Nick pulled a chair out from the table to wedge under the handle.

"I'm going to call the police."

"Let me explain."

The banging stopped and instead the man began scratching at the lock. A moment later there was silence.

Abby looked from the door back to Nick. "Is he gone?"

Nick shook his head.

"Is he drunk?"

Abby stood up and left the kitchen. Nick followed her into the hallway.

Light streamed through the glass panels of the front door. Nick was struck by a memory of standing on the doorstep waiting for her to answer the door. It wasn't their first date, but it had been early in their relationship. He remembered standing there filled with an unexpected fear that she would not answer the door. The two moments in time collided: the then and the now.

Nick heard the man's shuffling feet and his ragged in/out breathing. "Don't!" he started to say. A moment later a shadow fell across the glass.

"I'm going to tell him to leave."

The lock on the front door gave a loud snap as Abby opened it. Nick knew the dead man would have heard it too. Heard it and understood exactly what it meant.

Nick rushed forward as the door handle began to drop. He pushed Abby out of the way and put his shoulder to the door. On the wall of the corridor there was already a thin slice of sunlight.

The man pushed. Nick used all his weight to slam the door shut.

When he looked round Abby was staring at him. Everything in her body language screamed terror, but it was him she was afraid of, not the man outside.

She spoke slowly. Her voice dropped in volume and tone until she was whispering. "Please, Nick."

He held out his empty hands. Part of him was filled with the urge to grab her shoulders and shake her until she listened to him. He wanted to scream into her face to wake her up.

Abby backed away from him.

"Go to the window in the front room and look at him."

Her feet, slipping backwards over the hall runner, stuttered. Nick could almost read the thoughts on her face. There was a phone in the front room, in the corner next to the window.

He took a step backwards, held up his hands. "Do what you want, I'm not going to stop you. But just look at him. Take a proper look at him."

She turned and fled into the front room and Nick waited.

The dead man stood on the step, peering in through the glass of the door. The mottled pattern distorted his features. Two holes represented his eyes above a jagged smear which Nick assumed was his mouth. He was saying something, but the meaning of the words was impossible to make out.

The figure stepped away from the door and from the next room Nick heard a thud as the man thumped against the window of the front room. Abby shouted at him, loud and unintelligible.

When Abby returned to the corridor her skin was three shades paler. Her eyes were dark, almost black, the drawn skin around the sockets accentuating the shadows.

"What is he?"

"You believe me?" Nick asked.

Abby shrugged. "I thought he was going to break the window to get at me."

Before today he would have dismissed the idea – the dead walked around and stole what they wanted, but there was always a passivity to their actions. They stole with a touch. But this was different; fearing the dead man might punch through the window to take what he wanted did not seem unreasonable.

"He's dead," Abby said. It was a statement, not a question, but Nick nodded his head in agreement. Finally, she understood. He should have been relieved, except he was afraid her change in perspective came from the infection racing through her bloodstream.

The letterbox flapped open and closed quickly. A draft of air brought the stink of his decaying body into the hall.

"If I call the police..." Abby said.

"They'll move him on. And he'll come back."

Nick sat down in the hallway, his back pressed against the under-stairs cupboard and his feet resting against the far wall. After a moment Abby joined him, sitting crossways so her ankles were next to Nick's hips.

"How are you feeling?" Nick asked.

"Scared."

"No. I mean…" He couldn't think of any way to ask the question. "There was a woman with a child. One of those things touched her and now the girl is dead."

"And that thing wants to infect me?"

"It already has."

CHAPTER 16

Nick reached out to take hold of Abby's arm. Somewhere safe, between her elbow and her shoulder. She pulled away from him. For a second, he felt the warmth of her clothes beneath his fingertips and then it was gone.

"Don't," Abby said.

He leaned closer. "I need to look."

Abby pulled up the sleeve of her blouse. As far as Nick could see there was no sign of infection. Yet. He was aware of Abby's breath against his cheek. She was watching him, waiting for him to explain. He peered at the pale skin, almost praying he would find something he could use to convince her to believe him, but there was nothing.

"What is it?" Abby asked. Her voice trembled. Nick was desperate to gather her into his arms and hold her close. To comfort her and tell her everything was going to be alright, even if that was a lie. He touched her other shoulder and felt the fear running through her.

"You're shaking."

Abby tried to laugh. "No shit, Sherlock."

Nick laughed. It came out thin and weak.

"What is it?" Abby asked.

Nick looked at her arm again, pushing up the cuff of her blouse to reveal more skin. Was the area around her elbow a darker red? Maybe flushed with the beginnings of a rash? He assumed it was just his imagination, but the more he stared at her skin the easier it was to believe he could see something.

"Can you see anything?" he asked her.

"What?" Panic feathered her words. "What has he done to me?"

"I think..." Nick hesitated. He took a deep breath and tried to convince himself that it was just a small lie, and a lie for the best reason. Even if he couldn't see anything on her skin yet, the infection was there, burrowing through her body. It was just a matter of time before it erupted from her organs but if she was treated early maybe she could be cured.

Abby stared at her own arm. "I don't see anything."

"You need to know what you're looking for. See where your skin is red?" He pushed away his guilt. It was the right thing to do.

"How do I stop it?"

"I don't know."

"You have to know." He heard the panic in Abby's voice. "You have to tell me." Abby looked down at her arm. She held it in front of her as if it were no longer part of her body. Nick had the idea that if he offered to cut it off, she might agree.

"I'm sorry."

"Sorry isn't enough," Abby shouted at him.

There was no mistake now; the air was growing worse. He could taste it at the back of his throat, the soft, sweet stench of decay, like a barrel of fruit at the end of a hot summer's day. Nick wondered if she could smell it too.

Abby scrambled to her feet. She favoured the left side of her body, putting her weight onto her left hand as she struggled to stand up.

"You need to see someone. A doctor. You need to go to a hospital. They can sort it. They're scientists. You don't need to persuade them about what is happening, they'll be able to see it for themselves."

Abby shook her head, but Nick didn't give her the chance to say anything. He could see she was close to tears. "I'll take you," he insisted.

She swayed and for a second Nick was sure she was going to collapse. He watched the colour slip from her face until her cheeks were pure white. Her eyes stared at him but he could tell she wasn't actually looking at him. It only lasted a moment and then her cheeks filled with colour once more.

"Okay," she agreed in a small voice.

"We need to distract him."

"Maybe you could run out the back door and wave your hands until he comes for you?" Abby suggested. She smiled, to show it was a joke. Nick shrugged; he didn't have any better suggestions. He could see the man pacing back and forth, looking for a way inside.

"Why don't you have a garage?" Nick asked. "It would make everything so much easier."

"I'll remember that for the next time I get attacked."

Nick moved into the front room. Through the window he could see the man on the pavement, and just beyond him, Abby's pale yellow VW Polo. The dead man paced back and forth. He looked like a sickly lion, too weak to pounce and yet still dangerous, perhaps more so because he was hungry.

Abby arrived at Nick's shoulder.

"Who is he?" Her breath was light. It carried a soft hint of pungency and he wondered what caused the odour – if even now the disease was rotting inside her.

"I don't know. It doesn't matter."

"It matters to me," Abby said, her voice rising.

"I didn't mean that. I mean it could have been any of them."

"There's more?"

Nick nodded. He couldn't bring himself to admit it out loud. *There are hundreds.* All of them waiting for the chance to grab a few more days of life.

Abby looked out of the window. When she tried to slip her hand into his, Nick managed to draw back before she touched him.

CHAPTER 17

"Why did they choose me?"

Nick considered saying nothing. It was probably better that he didn't tell her. Definitely better. Keeping the secret was probably the best thing he could do.

"It's my fault," he said, but his mouth was so dry and his words were so quiet he was forced to repeat the confession before she heard him properly.

He stared at the man on the pavement and hated him. Before, fear had directed his actions, but before it had always been impersonal. When they had claimed people, Nick had been left with a dull sense that he should do something to stop them, but he had been frightened. He had always been frightened.

"Why?" Abby asked.

"They wanted to hurt me," Nick said. It felt like he had been dodging his duty ever since he was old enough to understand what *they* were. Accepting responsibility for Abby was such a small thing and yet it felt so hard.

"What did you do to them?"

"Nothing. I did nothing."

"So why punish you?" Abby asked. "Maybe it's just random. Maybe I was just the wrong person in the wrong place."

Nick shook his head. "No. He knew what he was doing when he claimed you. I saw him." It occurred to him how quickly Abby had come to accept the reality of the situation. He could have told her months ago; he hadn't needed to be alone.

Nick tapped on the window, and the dead man turned toward the noise.

"What did you do that for?"

"To see if he could hear us."

The man stumbled across the pavement until he was standing outside the front door. Nick waited until his silhouette covered most of the glass.

"Okay, go to the back door and bang on that."

Abby glared at him. "He's not going to fall for that trick."

"You have a better idea?"

"This is my life, Nick."

"I know." He tried to keep the heat out of his voice. The man was on the other side of the door. He could punch his hand through the glass and grab Abby. It wouldn't take much. "I'm doing the best I can."

She glared at him for a moment longer, as if searching for something to say, before storming through the corridor. A moment later the sound of her fist on the back door filtered through the house. Abby started shouting, howling like a dog.

The dead man at the door didn't move.

"Go on," Nick whispered. "It's her you want, not me. Go after her." He stepped back from the door and watched the shadow. The man didn't move.

He wanted to bang on the door to scare him away, but that would probably have the opposite effect. Instead, he retreated down the corridor until he reached the kitchen.

Abby paused. "It's not working?"

"I don't think so."

He looked along the length of the corridor. The dark shadow was still painted on the glass of the front door.

Abby reached down to the key in the lock.

"What are you doing?"

She shrugged. "Maybe he needs a little more incentive to come around here." She opened the door. A cool wind blew in and Nick was sure he could smell the stench of the dead man seep into the room.

"What if he comes for you?"

"That's exactly what I want him to do."

She stepped out into the back garden. "Hey," she called.

Nick glanced through the doorway and into the garden. The stink grew stronger. He checked over his shoulder; the shape at the front door had disappeared. "Okay, he's gone. Let's go for it."

"No," Abby said. "We need to give ourselves enough time to escape." She stepped onto the path and started to shake the wooden gate. "You still there?" she called.

"Come on," Nick said.

The gates sounded like bones rattling together. Abby slapped her palms flat on the wooden panels.

Nick heard the slurred footsteps of the man as he walked along the side of the house. He saw a mop of brown hair approach the gates and then the latch shook as the man tried to turn it.

"Okay, come on now. He's here," he said to Abby.

"Go back inside the house," she told him.

The stink made his eyes water. The man needed to feed; his hunger was palpable. The reek of the skin sloughing off his bones and the muscles wasting to jelly caused Nick to gag. He coughed. His eyes watered. He held a hand up to his mouth, but it did nothing to ward away the nausea.

He tripped back into the kitchen, losing his footing and almost landing on his back. He took two staggered steps backwards and put out a hand to steady himself. All the while Abby stood on the other side of the gate, baiting the dead man to come closer.

She retreated to the steps of the kitchen door.

"The gate isn't locked," Nick said.

"I know."

If he was quick, he might have time to shoot one of the bolts home and stop the thing from getting closer to them. He moved forward but already the gate was opening.

Abby stepped into the kitchen and stood in the doorway. Past her, Nick could just make out the gate swing on its hinges and a moment later the man shuffled into the garden. He took a step toward the house, his face wearing a slack grin. Two quick steps brought him within touching distance of Abby. She slammed the door and trapped the man's fingers between door and frame.

"I can't close the door," Abby said. She glanced back at Nick, a flash of sheer panic on her face.

I told you. I told you. But this wasn't the time. The man's fingers wriggled against the edge of the door.

He snatched up the broom propped up in the corner of the kitchen. He approached, the broom held out in front of him like a cheap Roman Gladiator.

"When I say open the door..."

Abby looked from him to the brush, and then back again. She nodded, her lips pressed into a thin line.

Nick drew in a breath. It tasted of death and decay. He tried to find a calmness within him but there was only a frantic need to get this thing done. He nodded, sharp, clear, before he could change his mind. Abby swept open the door. He charged at the man with the broom, planted it in his chest and pushed him off the steps and toward the gate. He let go of the broom and it clattered to the ground and Abby swept forward and slammed the door shut before the man had the chance to throw himself forward.

"Go out the front," Nick said.

Abby shook her head. "No, it's me he wants, isn't that right? You take my keys. Open the front door. I'll keep him here until you're ready."

Nick was poised to argue, except she was right. Still, hurrying away from her felt cowardly. He heard her snap the bolts on the door and then stand there calling to the man, taunting him.

The keys were tangled metal in his hand, and he fumbled with them, unable to separate them. He couldn't find the right key. He heard Abby at the back door and the stench of the dead was growing stronger. He forced himself to stop, to calm down. His hands were trembling but at least the wild panic had left his mind and he could concentrate on finding the key for the door. When the key turned, the snap of the lock sounded loud, but Nick thought the noise probably would not carry beyond the hallway.

He held the keys in the flat of his hand, picking out the right one for Abby's car. He eased open the door.

"Ready?" he shouted to her.

Abby rapped her knuckles on the door, inciting the man to a greater frenzy.

"Go," she shouted at Nick. It took him a moment to start moving, so Abby almost crashed into him in the narrow hallway. And then they were both outside.

CHAPTER 18

In the end he had to help her into the car. She settled into the passenger seat and her arm fell across her body. Nick noticed her wince and bite on her lower lip, but she didn't say anything. He leaned across to buckle her in and Abby held the seat belt away from her arm. As he leaned into her the smell of ripe decay hit him again and he swallowed the nausea. He closed the door and ran around the front of the car to get into the driver's seat.

"Take it easy," Abby told him. He raced the engine, his foot heavy on the accelerator. From the corner of his eye, he noticed Abby's response and decided it gave her something different to worry about.

"I've never driven your car before," he noted.

"I know."

It took fifteen silent minutes to reach the hospital. Nick parked in the drop off zone and helped Abby to the door. The smell of antiseptic rolled out from the building. Inside the door was an area filled with red and blue chairs; about a third of the chairs were already occupied. A man in his late fifties stood inside the doorway, perfectly dressed in a brown suit and red tie. He held a clipboard and Nick's first thought was that he was conducting market research.

"Are you okay, missy?" he asked Abby.

Nick winced, waiting for Abby to explain that she was not a missy, she was not even a miss. She was a mizz, or she was Abby. The tirade never came. She nodded.

"Don't worry, missy. They'll sort you out soon enough. If you have a quick word with Nurse Helen while I get your husband here to fill out a form." He pushed the clipboard into Nick's hands and put a hand on the small of Abby's back to propel her across the floor to a hatch where a woman in a white nurse's uniform scowled. Nick couldn't quite hear the conversation. He looked down at the form and recognised that apart from the most basic questions he wasn't able to answer much. He didn't know the name of Abby's doctor, he didn't know her national insurance number. When he next looked, Abby was gone. The man in the brown suit picked up another clipboard and returned to his post by the door.

"Where's Abby?" Nick asked. "Where have you taken her?"

"She's gone to triage. She shouldn't be too long."

Nick held out the clipboard. "I can't fill most of it in. I'm not her husband."

The man nodded at the hatch. "Hand it to her."

The nurse took the form and added it to a pile on the trolley to her right. "Take a seat," she said, and when Nick started to lower himself into the closest empty chair she barked out from her roost inside the hatch, "A blue chair! Blue chairs are for triage!"

He tried not to look at all the other people around him. People bound up with bandages around their hands and their arms, and with faces bright red and sweating with pain.

The hands of the clock above Nurse Helen's hatch were sluggish and more than once Nick checked his watch to confirm the passage of time. Occasionally a nurse in a blue smock would arrive through the double doors and announce a name and one of those waiting in chairs would answer the summons.

Finally, Abby came out of the double doors, the sleeve of her top rolled up over her shoulder. She was in conversation with one of the nurses and for a moment she paused in the doorway. When they finished speaking the nurse retreated through the doors and Abby made straight for the exit. Nick hurried from his chair, but she was on the pavement before he reached her.

"Well?"

Abby carried on walking. She started to roll her sleeve down, pulling her hand across her body.

"What did they say?" Nick asked.

Abby hunched her chin into her chest.

"Abby!"

She stopped and whirled on her heels to face him. "What?" she shouted. "What do you want me to say?"

"I want to know how you are."

"It's none of your business. None of this has anything to do with you."

"But..."

She started walking again, faster now. Harder. Her feet thumped against the pavement. Nick's first instinct was to let her go: She'd made her feelings clear enough. He stood and watched her walk as far as the crossing. She was still rolling down the sleeve of her top when she lurched into the road without looking. If a car had come around the corner, she would have been killed.

He started to run. He didn't shout, because calling for Abby to wait would be a waste of breath. He caught up with her on the far side of the street and for a moment he walked alongside her without saying anything. She didn't acknowledge him, except in the hunched shape of her shoulders which made it clear she was not prepared to talk.

"I'll get the car," he said. Abby didn't react – she simply arched her shoulders even further and carried on stomping away from the hospital. Nick wondered if her plan was simply to walk for the three hours it would take to get back home.

He touched her shoulder and felt a momentary resistance as she tried to pull away from him.

"I want to help," he told her.

Abby was silent. After a moment he realised she was crying.

"What have you done to me?"

"I'll get the car. Let me drive you home."

Abby nodded, and as Nick reached the car, he turned around to check and saw she had not moved from where he left her. Not even an inch.

CHAPTER 19

He had to fasten the seatbelt again, leaning across her body to clip it into the holder. By the time Nick had settled into the driving seat Abby had stopped crying. He reached down to turn the key in the ignition, and she spoke quietly, almost a whisper.

"They didn't see it. I think in the end they wrote me off as a ... what do they call it, the ones who pretend they're ill so they can get some attention? Munchausen's?"

"What do you mean?"

"They looked at my arm and they couldn't see anything wrong with it. The nurse spent a while probing my skin and asking me lots of questions, most of which had nothing to do with my arm. She made out she was just chatting to me, you know, how was I feeling and where did I live and did I have any friends or family in the area, but it felt like she was filing away all my answers so she could record them later."

"They do that."

"No, they don't, not like that. If you present with a broken arm they feel around and then send you for an x-ray and once they can see the bone is broken, they fix it. It's only when they can't find anything wrong with you, anything *physical,* that they start asking those questions."

Nick was silent. She was right. Of course, she was right.

He turned the key in the ignition and pulled out from the kerb. His driving was an exaggerated mime of carefulness, checking his mirrors, feathering the brakes. He concentrated on the physical requirements of the task, the push-pull of the steering wheel as he turned a corner, changing gear as he drove away from traffic lights. Abby's silence filled the space between them.

He saw one of *them* on the drive back to Abby's house. The woman was walking along the pavement down by Greenham Park. She looked healthy, hardly any sign of decay, so Nick assumed she had fed recently. Nick glanced across at Abby to see if she had noticed the dead woman, but she was staring down at the fingers on her right hand, as if she was watching for the disease's progress through her bones.

Nick parked outside Abby's house. He left the engine running as he turned in his seat. "I can't see him."

"Maybe he was never here," Abby said.

"What do you mean?"

She pressed the fingers of her right hand into the skin of her arm. "Tell the truth. You made it up?"

He hesitated and Abby noticed. "You did? You put me through hell."

"I..." Nick started to say, but he couldn't find the words to explain. He wanted to point out that she was in danger. Did he make up the infection? He truly believed it was in her; just because it wasn't visible yet, didn't mean he was wrong.

"Get out," Abby said.

"He could still be hanging around."

"Who was he, one of your mates? Why are you doing this?"

Abby struggled to open the door herself and when he leaned across, she beat him away. "I can do it." He noticed she'd already unclipped the seat belt and her face was filled with colour from the exertion. She lurched out of the car, her stilted movements so like one of the dead.

She snatched the keys from his hand and opened the door to her house, leaving the car door wide open behind her. Nick closed the door and followed her up the path. At the doorstep, Abby waited just inside the threshold.

"Where do you think you're going?" she asked.

"I can't leave you like this."

"Why not?"

Nick clenched and unclenched his fist. Clenched and unclenched his fist. If the dead man was in front of him now, he wondered how much damage he would be able to inflict on him, and damn the consequences. Damn the possibility he would become infected.

He was desperate to tell Abby not to give up, that there had to be some way to make this better. His silence dragged on. Too long.

"That's what I thought," she said. Her voice cracked on the last word.

It reminded him of all the times he had cowered from the dead. At the time it had seemed the only sane thing to do.

"You have to believe," he said.

"Who are you trying to convince, me or you?"

She wouldn't let it go. She wouldn't accept he'd made a mistake. He was trying to help her - didn't she get that?

Anger rose like a flash flood and he drowned in it. There was a moment when he had no understanding of who he was or what he said. Just a moment, but it scared him, and when he came back to himself, he was marching away from the doorway, determined that he would not look back. Because none of this was his fault.

He turned the corner and carried on walking. And still the rage did not leave him. It simmered away inside, hot as lava and hard as stone.

Chapter 20

By the time he got home he was already an hour late for work, so he called and told Mark he was sick, hopefully nothing serious, probably back tomorrow. He hung up before Mark had a chance to start asking inane questions about doctor's notes and reports and deadlines.

He sat for ten minutes staring at the bare wall of the flat, waiting for Abby to call. When the phone didn't ring, he stepped onto the balcony and looked down on the cityscape. The sky was a blaze of orange which added to the sense that the last few days had been a dream. Or a nightmare. Everything since he had stood in the Market Square and watched the dead man follow Marjorie Hamilton into the alley, all of it existed nowhere except inside his mind. The burning skyline proved that.

He called his father and when there was no response, he left a message. "Dad. It's getting worse." He hesitated, unsure what else he could say to persuade his father to help. He contemplated another lie, this time suggesting he had become infected himself. He wondered if family would mean more, but in the end he kept to the truth because he was afraid if he lied about an infection his father might still ignore it, and he wasn't sure how he would respond to that rejection.

He left a message for Abby. A message for his father. Waited 30 minutes. Left a message for Abby. A message for his father.

Time circled in on itself and became irrelevant. It could have been minutes or hours or days. It could have been a single second twisted into a Mobius strip. No beginning and no end.

His mobile phone rang. It shivered in his cupped hand. *Abby?* He checked the screen for the caller ID: *Work.* He rejected the call. The last thing he needed right now was a conversation with Mark Hanscomb.

As the daylight faded, the houses began to light up. From five storeys up they looked like accessories to a toy train set. Nothing was real. Down on the pavement, smudges of darkness moved amongst the trees. People hurried home from work. A group huddled together beside a bus stop: Students heading into town, Nick thought. He watched as they tried to throw a green bag onto the roof of the bus shelter.

It wasn't fair, that was the hardest part. The child in the alley had been chosen because... well just *because*, there was no logic to it. The dead man had taken Abby because he knew it would cause pain. As a warning? To punish him for daring to get involved? There were so many others they could have claimed. They could have taken Mark – Nick laughed to himself at the idea. *Yeah, they should have taken Mark Hanscomb.*

The students at the bus stop cheered, and when Nick looked down, he saw the green bag was now lodged on the shelter's roof. One lad was clambering onto the shoulders of a friend to retrieve it.

It should have been his boss. Or Pete who sat in the corner of the office doing the accounts and picking his nose when he thought no one was looking. It could have been Sally, who Nick had once asked out on a date way, way back when he had first started at the company, and she had looked at him like his proposal had been truly degrading. Or Bob, yeah, it should have been Bob in Sales.

Nick leaned over the edge of the balcony and rested his arms on the railing. He imagined leading one of the dead men up the stairs into his office, spreading out his arms and saying; 'They're all yours. Personally, I'd start with Hanscomb but you won't find much life in him so you might need to take another few to fill your quota.' He smiled at the idea.

The air brakes of a bus dragged him back to reality. There was a cheer from the group of lads as one of them hooked his arm onto the roof and pulled down the bag just as the rest disappeared into the bus.

Nick went back inside and sat on the settee. He tried Abby's number again but wasn't surprised when there was no answer. He just had to wait until... until she accepted she needed him or it was too late to help her, whichever came first.

CHAPTER 21

He asked the taxi driver to drop him at the end of the road. The man glanced at him in the rear-view mirror and Nick understood the request sounded suspicious, but it was too late for an alternative. If he'd given more thought to his plans, he would have named a street at the edge of Abby's estate, but he was making it up as he went along, driven by the need to do something, even though he had no idea what that could be.

There was an awkward pause and then the driver unlocked the door after Nick handed over the fare. He left him at the side of the road and hurried away and Nick could hear him writing his own comments for when the journalists came: *I thought he was a bit odd. He didn't want to tell me where he was going. He had a shifty look about him.*

Once the road was empty, Nick walked towards Abby's house. Everything about it screamed that it was a bad idea, but he'd come to the conclusion it was probably the least-worst option open to him. He'd tried calling and that made no difference. What did she expect him to do, just pretend it wasn't happening?

He couldn't. He'd tried. That was his dad's approach to the whole thing.

He slowed down as he got closer to the house. It had only been twelve hours so there was no reason why it should look any different to when he had left Abby that morning, but he still inspected it carefully for signs of any change. He wasn't sure quite what he was expecting to find: broken windows, the front lawn wrecked? The house was quiet and settled and exactly the same as all the other properties up and down the street.

On the other side of the road a tall Leylandi offered a sense of protection and he stood beneath it and continued his observations. The curtains were drawn, but then Abby had a habit of leaving them closed. That meant nothing in and of itself. There were no lights on, but it was still early. Her car was outside the house and that was the strongest indicator she was home. It was possible she could have taken a taxi or had a friend come by to pick her up, possible but not probable. More likely she had come home from the office and was now holed up inside her home. Or maybe she had never ventured out. Maybe after he had left, she had locked the door and called in sick. That would explain the drawn curtains and the sense of stillness which settled over the house.

There was no sign of the dead man. Nick reminded himself that the absence didn't mean anything. He could have returned to his grave and intended to visit Abby later in the evening. Just because he wasn't there, it didn't mean he hadn't already fed.

From his vantage point he could see the front and side of the house, and if he hadn't witnessed the man climb over the fence to get to Abby, he would probably have been content to stand there and keep watch. Nick peeled away from the hedge and crossed the street. He checked behind him and sure enough the curtains opposite twitched; the Neighbourhood Witch had retreated, but not quickly enough.

He walked down the side of the house and let himself in the back gate. A sense of déjà vu overcame him, only this time he didn't think Abby would be welcoming him inside her home.

The garden was empty. He turned around to find Abby staring at him through the kitchen window. Her lips created a perfect circle of surprise, but the expression was immediately replaced with anger. She was shouting at him even through the back door. He couldn't hear what she was saying, but the rage exploded as soon as they were face to face.

"What are you doing here?"

"I came to check you were okay."

He replied automatically, without even properly processing the question. And then he stopped listening because he was looking at Abby, really looking at her. It was less than a day since he had last seen her, but that was impossible. Her eyes were dark pits, circled with brown and grey skin. He could see the bones in her cheeks cutting against her skin. He looked to her hand, which rested on the door, and saw that her fingers were skin and bones. It looked like she'd spent a month on a fad-diet and was now little more than a skeleton wrapped inside a bag of skin. She stopped shouting at him and even though she was just standing there she was wheezing; he could hear each laboured breath her body produced.

"He's been back." It was a statement rather than a question and Abby flinched when he said it, but there was no way she could deny the fact; he had been back and he had fed.

She wore a grey tracksuit top, black jogging bottoms. There were silver hairs on the shoulders of the tracksuit. Not just one or two strands, whole clumps of her hair had fallen out.

Nick had no idea what to ask. *What did he do to you?* He just whispered her name.

"I told you to stay away," she screeched at him. Her voice broke. Her lungs didn't have the air to power her words and she fell silent.

"I need to get you to the hospital."

"No."

"But this time..."

"No."

She blinked, paper-thin eyelids shuttering grey eyes.

He pulled out his phone and started to dial: 999.

"There's no point," Abby said. The anger faded from her voice. Now there was just resignation. His thumb rested above the call icon on the phone. The paramedics would see Abby and they would understand she was sick. She would be in a hospital. Cared for. Safe.

"They can't stop him. They'll just patch me up, send me out, and then he'll be back again." She paused, dry lips pressed together. "Think about the Quals, Nick."

It took him a moment to understand what she was saying.

"He came as soon as you left." Even though there was probably no intended accusation in Abby's words, they triggered a fresh surge of guilt. *As soon as you left. When you abandoned me.* Reminding Abby that she had sent him away did not feel appropriate.

"Let me help. Let me stay here. Look after you. Keep him away."

Abby shook her head, another clump of silvered hair drifted onto her shoulders.

"Maybe I don't deserve to be saved."

There was no response to that. Nick searched for one but came up empty.

"Let me go."

He wondered whether his mother had said something similar. Abby would never give up. She was the sort of person who would fight even when there was no hope. So, it wasn't her talking, it was the infection.

He couldn't argue with a sickness, any more than he was able to argue with the dead man. He bowed his head and turned around. As he passed through the garden gate he closed it softly behind him, and as he did, he heard the kitchen door fall shut.

The Neighbourhood Witch was waiting for him at the kerb, standing next to Abby's car. She was a woman in her early twenties in a loose T-shirt, with a narrow, pretty face. He stood for a moment and realised that in his mind he had painted her as a wizened old crone who was too sad and lonely to mind her own business.

"What's wrong with her?" she asked.

"What do you know?"

"She hasn't left the house since you brought her back this morning. There was a man hanging around; a tramp. Dirty brown jacket and ripped trousers. He looked like he hadn't washed in weeks. I tried to chase him away and then when he wouldn't leave, I rang Timothy."

"Timothy?"

"My PCSO. He came as soon as he could, but the man was gone by then."

"If he comes again then call the police straight away."

"Who is he?"

Nick paused. Was it worth telling her? How would she react? He wondered if the best way to protect Abby from the dead man was to shout about him, or if that would just mean he would be locked away.

"Someone who wants to hurt Abby."

The woman assessed him for a minute. He felt her scrutiny of his words went beyond their content, as if she was deciding whether to trust him based on how he looked as much as what he said. He tried to smile, but then remembered Abby often said his forced smile looked predatory.

The woman nodded her head slowly as she came to a decision. "I'm Susannah. If I see him around, I'll call Timothy."

"Thank you."

He gestured with his phone. "Take my number. Ring me if anything happens."

It took her a moment to agree. Nick was conscious he looked a little ragged around the edges. He couldn't remember the last time he'd shaved but he resisted the temptation to stroke his chin to check the state of his stubble.

"The same goes for you, too. Abby just needs a chance to rest without all of you clamouring around her."

He thought about arguing with her, but what was the point? She was probably right.

CHAPTER 22

Nick wound the chain around the cemetery gates and fastened it with a padlock. He stepped back and leaned on the end of the broom to admire his work; the steel sheen of the new chain contrasted with the dull black of the old gates.

"I won't fail," Nick called into the cemetery. He would ensure Abby's predator remained trapped inside, unable to prey upon her.

The dead drifted into view, emerging from the gloom. When the wind changed direction Nick caught their scent and had to turn away to avoid retching.

Nick stood outside. The uneven cobblestones pressed up into the soles of his shoes. He wrapped his fingers around the iron railings and peered into the darkness beyond. He tried to spot Abby's predator from all the figures trapped inside the cemetery, but he was not visible. Not yet.

Night air caressed the back of his neck and brushed his cheeks. A teenage girl in a leather biker jacket over a tattered white T-shirt made directly for the exit and only stopped when she was a few feet in front of Nick. She glared at Nick but said nothing. Decay had eaten away half of her face so he wasn't sure if she could actually see him. Her long blonde hair looked as dry as straw. She licked her lips with a black tongue and when she lurched forwards and thrust her hands between the railings it was so unexpected Nick tripped over in his haste to escape her.

She tested the gates, bony fingers wrapped around the iron. They clanged like a prison cell. The girl stood on the apron of tarmac inside of the cemetery, peering out. He could smell her rotting body on the wind, and even when he stepped away, he could taste her at the back of his throat. He spat a lump of saliva and phlegm into the gutter but it didn't take away the taste.

On the road behind him, late night taxis thundered past to the suburbs and all points north. Their headlights flashed across the cemetery, illuminating gravestones and the rotting faces of corpses.

Nick took out his phone and searched the contacts for Abby's neighbour. *Susannah.* He dialled and she picked up immediately.

"All quiet?" he asked.

"Not a sound," she reported.

He waited, trying to decide what else he could ask. He wondered what Abby would think if she learned he was collaborating with the Neighbourhood Witch to spy on her. It was for a good cause, he reminded himself. Even if she didn't understand, they were doing it for her benefit.

He hung up without saying anything else. After a while, when the chill was seeping into his bones, he started to walk the perimeter of the cemetery. The iron railings bordered three sides and a high stone wall made up the fourth. For some reason Nick was unable to properly understand, he felt most anxious when he was behind the wall and the graves and their occupants were hidden from view.

From the other side of the wall he heard the rustle of their footsteps as they trudged through the grass and the drifts of fallen leaves that had lain there since last autumn. He heard voices, but there was no sense of a conversation; rather it was as if everyone in the cemetery was trying to talk at once and there was no one there to listen.

He passed beyond the wall and kept the cemetery's railings on his left as he walked. He used the handle of the broom like a walking stick, the wooden tip clacking against the cold pavement.

When he returned to the iron gates, he was certain the woman had not moved.

"What do you want?" he asked.

Her only answer was the hunger that rolled off her in ugly waves.

He pressed against the iron bars of the fence. It felt like he might slip between them and find himself inside the cemetery, with nothing to protect him from the dead.

Nick started to walk another circuit of the cemetery's perimeter. He walked faster, like a spaceship trying to escape the gravity of a planet, and when he returned to the entrance gates the woman was still there.

He carried on walking. Faster. His head bent down to the ground. Out of the corner of his eye he watched the spaces between the gravestones. The figures on the other side of the bars milled around the edges of the cemetery. A man with a dull red Puffa jacket lifted his hands up to the fence but Nick rapped his knuckles with the broom handle and when the man tried a second time, he planted the head of the broom into the centre of the man's chest and pushed him away. Each time the man approached, Nick repelled him, until finally he turned back and slipped into the darkness in the middle of the cemetery.

Sweat ran down Nick's spine. His legs ached. Muscles spasmed across his back. His eyes scratched with tiredness. Still, he walked. One of the creatures kept pace with him, hurdling gravestones and dodging around stone crypts to remain beside him: A teen with a dirty tracksuit top shredded into strips.

"Go away!"

The dead teen stayed with him.

"Leave me alone," Nick shouted into the graveyard.

The girl watched him with blank eyes. Her mouth hung open, like a pike trying to breathe.

Nick reached the wall and leaned against the cool stone. He heard scrabbling sounds from the other side as the dead girl climbed the brick. He waited a moment. The scratching sound stopped.

He ran back to the entrance and at some point the dead girl faded away, as if she had never been there in the first place, and there was only the woman there, staring at him.

Behind the woman, Nick saw shapes emerging from the darkness of the night. A young girl in a yellow raincoat. An elderly man clutching a panama hat tightly in his fist. A young man with a brown suit, yellow tie, and a gaping hole in his jaw.

"Stay away," Nick shouted at the last man. "You keep away from her!"

Abby's dead man changed direction and walked to the section of fencing where Nick stood. As he moved closer, he stumbled over the uneven ground and dropped to one knee. For a moment the back of his neck was perfectly exposed and the white knuckles of his spine punctured the grey skin. Nick considered unlocking the padlock and rushing into the cemetery to club the man while he was down. He got as far as taking the key from his pocket before he peered around at the other dead crowded near the gate. Maybe he could push through them to reach Abby's killer. Maybe. It was possible one of the dead would infect him and he considered whether he was willing to take the risk. By the time the padlock key was back in his pocket the dead man had regained his feet and was almost at the fence.

Nick raised the broomstick and when the man curled his fingers around the iron railings Nick brought the wood down on the man's fingers. The dead man snatched his hands away and snarled at Nick, black liquid slipping out of the hole in his jaw.

"I can do this every night," Nick warned him. "As long as it takes."

The dead man paid no heed to Nick's words. He shuffled along the railings until he reached the gate, where he pressed his hands through to grab hold of the padlock. Nick raised his broomstick but held it above his head; the dead man's fingers would be no match for the lock.

Nick stepped up until he was opposite the gate. The man could possibly have reached through the bars and grabbed him, but he was focussed solely on trying to break the padlock. The silver surface of the lock was smeared with black blood and fragments of skin that sloughed off the man's decaying fingers. He could hear the bone scrape against the metal surface.

The man glanced up and saw Nick watching him. "Let me out."

"To feed on Abby? You can stay in there until you rot."

The man shook the gates with both hands. The gates were over a hundred years old, but they seemed sturdy enough to last another century. The action reminded Nick of a caged monkey in a zoo. He grinned at the image and that seemed to inflame the man. "I'll take you, too!"

"But you can't," Nick said, "That's the way it works. So, I'll keep you in there until you're nothing more than the pile of bones you're supposed to be."

The man howled. His lungs didn't have the strength to give the anguish any real power, and after a few seconds he fell into a quiet wheeze.

"Go back," Nick said. "Lie down. You're not getting out."

The dead man attacked the gates again. It was fully an hour before he slipped away into the darkness of the cemetery. Defeated.

CHAPTER 23

The ragged engine of a van woke Nick from a fitful sleep which seemed infected by dreams that washed away in the sunlight. His back muscles ached and his spine felt like it had been rubbed raw. He opened his eyes to see the white council van parked up on the kerb just in front of the gates. A young woman dropped down from the driver's seat. Dirty jeans and a ripped black jacket. Her blonde hair was pushed back beneath a cap. She walked over to the gates and spent a moment inspecting the new padlock.

Finally, she turned to him. "You did this?"

"You can't let them escape."

She looked tired. "Stop pissing about."

"If they get out…" Nick watched her expression, trying to decide how much she already knew about the dead. Trying to decide if she was in league with them. "They infected my girlfriend. I can't let them get to her again."

"I don't have the time for you lot." She turned her back on him and reached through the open door to retrieve a set of bolt cutters. "If you do it again, I'm calling the police."

She muttered under her breath as she cut the chain and then pushed the gates open wide. Once she was back behind the wheel, she steered the van into the cemetery and slowly down the right-hand pathway, the edges of the van only a few inches from the stone markers of the graves.

Nick struggled to sit upright and then used the broom handle to lever himself into a standing position. His clothes felt cold and damp, although there had been no rain while he was asleep.

The cemetery looked still. He wondered how long the peace would last. How long before the dead discovered the gates were open again and they were free to go out and feed? He gripped the broomstick tightly. He would try and stop them all, but if there were too many, there was really just one he needed to keep within the grounds.

Behind him, a steady stream of cars flowed into the city. He checked his watch; just after six am. He'd had maybe two hours sleep, hardly any more than that. He had a memory of waking when Abby's dead man returned at some point in the night and shook the gates, but on that occasion Nick had not even bothered to stand up to confront the ghoul.

He was aware he was now standing on the street corner, armed with a broom, keeping guard over the exit to the cemetery. *None shall pass*, he thought to himself and laughed at the idea. He wondered what the sleepy-eyed early morning drivers would make of the scene, or if they would catch a glimpse of him from the corner of their vision and dismiss it as a mirage.

The sludge-scrape of shoes against the ground signalled the approach of the dead. From the depths of the cemetery, they rose up between the graves and trudged towards the open gates.

Nick raised the broom handle until it was level with his shoulder, as if he were a baseball player ready for the first pitch. He scanned the path in front of him. A teenage kid was stumbling up on the left. An elderly woman was walking with impressive speed through the middle, steering her way between headstones. From a distance Nick would not even have been sure she was one of the dead if it had not been for the fact that no one other than the park keeper had entered the cemetery since she opened the gates.

He tensed his muscles.

Not surprisingly, the elderly woman reached him first. Instead of swinging wildly at the figure he waited until she was almost upon him, and then pressed the end of the broomstick into her chest to turn her away.

The woman tried to grab the wooden stick and Nick snatched it from her and pressed the end into her rib cage. From just a few feet away she smelled of boiled cabbage and sour eggs. Black beetles skittered across her scalp. Her gums were drawn back to reveal her jaw, with holes where teeth should have been.

"You're not going out," Nick said. He was mindful of the teenage kid still a way off to the left. Quickly he pulled the broom handle back and held it in two hands to use it as a quarterstaff to drive the woman back until she lost her footing and fell to the ground. He felt her finger bones snag at his clothing, but she did not touch his skin.

He ran to the teenage kid and repeated the move, and while the boy was on the ground the elderly woman was rising once again. He pushed her back another ten feet until she was level with the sign marking the opening hours of the cemetery. He alternated between the pair of them, pushing them deeper into the graveyard – attacking one and then the other, always keeping an eye beyond them for any others who might be making their way to the gates.

By the time the two gave up and turned around, Nick was lathered in sweat. He plucked his T-shirt away from his skin and brushed the hair from his face, and took up his position at the gates, ready for the next arrivals.

Before eight o'clock he'd hidden the broomstick down by the wall and covered it in leaves, knowing that walking around the graveyard in full view with the stick would only result in a phone call to the police. Instead, he stole a pair of gardening gloves from the back of the Council van and tucked the cuff of his jacket beneath the gloves and continued his war against the dead. Up close and personal.

He guessed he was successful in turning back about half of the dead who tried to leave the graveyard to feed, and pragmatically he accepted that most of those who turned around, probably came back later and tried again. He kept expecting them to rise up and rush him as one, and if they did then he wouldn't last more than a few seconds. Instead, they came singularly, walking up the hill from the depths of the graveyard and making their solitary attempts to escape.

Abby's dead man staggered up the hill towards the cemetery's gates. Nick recognised his brown suit and yellow tie. The darkness shaded half of his face. He stumbled between the graves, holding out his hands to steady himself against a memorial of a stone angel.

Nick allowed the dead woman he had been tackling to pass beyond him. He ran across the graves and met the man while he was still struggling to reach the path. He caught him in the centre of his chest with both hands and pushed him back so he lost balance and crashed to the ground.

Close up, the dead man's face was the grey of ash. The stench of decay was almost overpowering. It lodged at the back of Nick's throat and he found himself tasting old blood and rotting tissues with each breath he took.

The man scrabbled to his feet, and as soon as he was upright Nick started to push him deeper into the cemetery. It was almost too easy – the dead man was unable to put up any resistance. His bones were like thin twigs that snapped under the slightest pressure.

Not long now, he thought. Given the state of the dead man, he guessed that in another couple of days he would be too weak to stand. Abby would be safe.

See, Dad! Nick thought to himself. *I can do something.* He tucked the idea away for the future.

The dead man's hands flailed weakly against Nick. Raw bones scratched at his clothes and a few times Nick felt the brief touch of skin against skin. Enough to infect him? He wasn't sure – even if the dead man was able to draw life from someone other than Abby, the contact was fleeting.

He drove the dead man in front of him as the path dipped down into the central bowl of the cemetery. The man staggered and dropped to his knees. By the time Nick was out of sight of the road, the dead man had allowed himself to be herded back to where he had come from. Nick turned him around, gave him a final push, and then sat on the edge of a stone tomb as the man staggered away.

Nick waited ten minutes. Time to catch his breath and let his body cool from the exertion. Time to be sure the dead man was truly gone, before he trudged back up the hill to continue his sentry duty at the exit gates. He had no doubt the man would be back, but next time he would be even weaker, even easier to deal with. The nightmare was finally coming to an end.

CHAPTER 24

The people around him blurred. It was like staring through a fog. Everything was distorted: the people, the headstones, the railings. He wiped his eyes with the back of his hand and it made a little improvement, at least for a moment. He looked across the graveyard and he could distinguish the row of houses on the street behind the railings.

He heard the dead muttering to themselves as they made the journey up to the gates. He heard the rush of traffic behind him, punctuated with the rare squeal of a police siren. Silence rushed in, muting the world. And then the next wave of sound crashed down upon him.

Through the noise came the sound of the dead man. His footsteps, solid and deliberate. He came closer. Nick heard his voice and realised he could understand what he was saying. The voice sounded like a handful of gravel crushed together, rough edges scraping against stone.

The figure came into view, not a dead man, but a young girl in a yellow dress.

The girl from the alley. Nick remembered her mother's name from the article, Marjorie. Her daughter's name came after: Jane Hamilton. Her dress was dirty and ragged around the hem. Splashes of mud or blood stained the front of her clothing. There was a slight shadow around her eyes. Her features were gaunt, exposing the ridges of cheekbones. But more than anything else, she looked hungry.

Nick felt the breath in his lungs turn cold. "What do you want?"

The young girl grinned; a crooked smile that made her look ugly and old. "I don't want to be alone."

Nick looked into the girl's eyes and saw nothing – not even his reflection. They were pools of dull black. She bared her throat to him. Her wrinkled skin was stained with earth.

Grave dirt, Nick thought. He imagined her breaking out of her coffin and clawing her way up to reach the surface, like a diver returning from the depths. He glanced at her hands – the skin on her fingertips was ripped open. Most of her fingernails had been lost.

There was no way she could have been buried so soon, and yet here she was.

"Touch me," she said. There was nothing sexual in the invitation, just the bold threat: *touch me and take away the rot and the worms and the grave dirt beneath my fingernails.* The girl laughed as Nick recoiled.

Her hand raked the air in front of his face. Nick jerked his head away. *That was close.*

And what would happen if she succeeded? A quiet death in the night like Jane Hamilton? A mysterious disease no one could treat, like his mother? He sensed the young girl needed to find someone new to feed on. The terror of infection almost paralysed him and the tattered gardening gloves he wore seemed little protection. Just the slightest touch and he would be claimed.

He hated the inevitability of it. He was completely powerless. The dead took what they wanted and no one could stop them.

Ahead of him a group of children looked like they were out on a school trip. There were ten of them, shouting and laughing and bouncing against each other as they walked. Nick wanted to warn them to be quiet, not to attract attention. They had to be careful in this city.

On the far side of the road a traffic warden paused to check the details on a ticket plastered to the windscreen of a white van. An old woman with bright red hair and a yellow handbag as large as a briefcase stood peering through the window of a second-hand guitar shop.

There was no one in charge of the children, Nick realised immediately. There was no one responsible.

Jane ran toward the group of children. Her gait was uneven, but Nick understood instantly that they didn't notice she was there.

"Run," he shouted.

The traffic warden looked up from the car. The old woman turned around to check what was happening. One of the children in the gang turned her head in Nick's direction but immediately dismissed the shout as nothing to do with her.

Jane looked at Nick with disdain.

Why shouldn't she ignore me? Nick thought. *What can I do to stop her?*

He pushed Jane Hamilton back and she staggered but kept her balance. She was stronger than Abby's dead man. She stepped forward, challenging Nick to try and hold her back and instantly he knew his tactic would not work this time.

He turned and ran towards the pack of schoolchildren.

The group broke before he reached them. It reminded him of pigeons scattering before a toddler. Schoolchildren in crimson blazers ran in every direction.

Marjorie's daughter turned to scowl at him and then changed her direction to follow one of the boys.

The boy fled. The girl in the yellow dress followed. And Nick chased them both. The boy ran along the path, deeper into the cemetery. He glanced behind him, his face drawn in confusion rather than fear.

Nick realised how it looked to anyone watching: the man chasing the two children. No one would notice anything different about the girl in the yellow dress.

The boy ducked down a path and glanced over his shoulder. When he saw the strange man was still following him, he sped up.

An ache was already growing in Nick's side. Sweat ran down his brow and into his eyes. He wanted to stop running. But Nick understood that if he stopped running the boy would stop too, and Jane would reach him in seconds.

"Leave me alone!" the boy shouted before turning off the path and running between the rows of graves. He cut a path across the plots until he stood on the cobblestone circle just outside of the cemetery gates. He paused to look back, and then ran across the road.

Marjorie's daughter hesitated at the gates. By the time Nick reached the same spot the boy had disappeared. The yellow dress faltered and then stopped.

Nick slowed to a walk. The pain in his side had swollen. He pressed his hand against the spot and the pain lessened slightly.

Cars flashed by on the other side of the railings. He tried not to imagine what might have happened if the boy had misjudged the traffic as he ran across the road in his panic to escape.

The girl had not moved. She stood in the middle of the pavement. When she turned around Nick discovered she was crying. Tear tracks ran down grubby cheeks, washing thin lines into her skin. They served to emphasize how dirty she was. Beneath the patina of grave dirt her skin was grey. She rubbed the back of her hand across her eyes and smudged the dirt over her cheeks. She looked like the survivor from a disaster; a war refugee or the homeless victim of a flash flood. She was the poster child of a hundred charity appeals Nick had watched over the years.

This is my fault, he thought.

He stopped short of where she stood: she might have looked a pitiful sight, but she was dangerous.

"I hate you," she said.

"I can't let you take him."

"There will be others."

Nick shrugged. "Maybe I can't stop all of you, but that boy is safe."

"Because of you."

He heard the disdain in her voice but chose to ignore it; he had saved the boy. At that moment the pain in his side meant nothing. He leaned forward. His chest ached from the need to get more air into his lungs, but it was a welcome pain. He grinned at Marjorie's daughter. "You weren't expecting that?"

"It doesn't matter."

He could feel her hunger. *Doesn't matter?* He wanted to shout at her that of course it mattered. He'd made a difference.

The girl came within touching distance and he was sure she was going to reach out a hand and claim him. She needed to feed. Her cheekbones were sharp and her skin was pulled tight across the bones in her face. Her eyes were sunken pits where shadows flourished. She reeked of death and hunger.

He did not move. In part it was because he was no longer afraid, but just being unafraid was not enough to remain standing opposite the girl. He felt alive, truly alive. He had spent too much time being frightened of the dead.

The girl reached out her hand and brushed the edge of his jacket. "You can't stop me," she whispered. "Not forever."

"Maybe just for today," Nick said to her, and when he pushed her back through the gates and propelled her in the direction of the middle of the cemetery, she put up no resistance.

CHAPTER 25

The dead were persistent. Nick's stomach ached with hunger, but he couldn't afford to leave his position next to the gates. The dead bubbled up from the lower reaches of the cemetery like marsh gas through mud. Each time he sat down to rest he might get five minutes respite before the next body came staggering up the hill to try and get past him. He didn't stop them all; at one point he had to choose between the kid in the SuperDry hoodie and an old woman in a floral pink dress. He chose to stop SuperDry Hoodie; for no good reason except a sense that the old woman was going out to feed on someone she had already infected while maybe the kid was looking to find a new claim.

The girl in the yellow dress came back and Nick turned her away again. The woman from the Council drove past in the van and glared at Nick. She looked like she might stop and question him on why he was hanging around the cemetery all day, but although she slowed to a crawl when she reached the gates, the truck didn't stop. As she turned out of the gates Nick peered into the back of the van, as if expecting to see a huddle of the dead hiding there like prisoners breaking out in a movie. The back of the truck was empty. He didn't know if they didn't have the wit or the strength to escape.

After the third time when he jerked awake after falling into a doze, he refused to sit down but instead walked tight circles underneath the arches of the gates. It reminded him of time spent talking to Abby on his mobile, pacing the stairwell outside his offices. The memory hurt. It felt impossibly distant, and there was a real sense that Nick would never get back to that life. Even if he managed to starve the man in the brown suit until he was no longer a threat to Abby, those innocent days when he could ignore his responsibilities towards the dead were gone.

The realisation birthed anger bordering on hate. He aimed it at the man in the brown suit but some of it deflected onto Abby, onto his dad, onto himself. No one was truly without fault in this mess.

He took out his mobile and called his father, and when it went to voicemail, he left a long incoherent message he was certain his father would simply delete as soon as he recognised the voice.

The woman from the Council came back and this time she stopped the van in the middle of the gateway and stepped onto the cobblestones. She took three steps in Nick's direction, so he retreated across to the far side of the road. He thought she was going to pursue him. She went as far as standing on the kerb and watching him across the roofs of the traffic, before retreating into the van and disappearing into the depths of the graveyard.

He watched the dead walk out of the cemetery unchallenged. SuperDry hoodie and then Jane Hamilton. The temptation to cross the road and push them back amongst the graves was strong, but Nick accepted he had one job – stop the man in the brown suit.

He was sure more than one of the dead glanced in his direction as they stepped out of the cemetery. There was a sneering challenge to their looks, as if they gloated at the fact that he could no longer restrain them. He considered crossing the road to tell the council worker what he was doing, and how she should be supporting him in protecting the city, but it was a gamble he wasn't prepared to take. Maybe it would work, or maybe he would spend the rest of the day explaining himself in a police interview room, while the guy in the brown suit tracked down Abby.

He tried calling his father again and got the same straight-to-voicemail response. When he called Abby's phone, he no longer had the option to record a message. He paced the pavement and stared at the gates hard enough that, if it were possible, his willpower alone would have kept them closed. Instead, the dead kept on coming; he saw SuperDry return, skipping across the cobblestones, his face flushed with life. Occasionally genuine visitors to the cemetery would arrive and Nick had to bite down on the urge to shout out warnings to them.

Below the sound of the traffic, he heard the dragging footsteps of the dead as they made their way back to the cemetery after a feeding. The stink of decay still hung around them, even once their skin was bright with life and their injuries were healed, as if the truth of their death was hidden just below the surface.

The man in the brown suit walked up the hill, towards the cemetery.

"No!" Nick shouted. Even across four lanes of traffic and the noise of the city his cry carried to the dead man, who turned in his direction and grinned. The man glistened with health.

How? Nick started to ask himself as he ran across the road, weaving between the moving vehicles. He reached the gates of the cemetery just before the dead man. "How did you get out?" Nick asked.

The dead man's skin glowed. The crack in his skull was gone. His eyes were a brilliant blue.

"How much of Abby did you take?" Nick asked.

"All of her."

CHAPTER 26

Susannah answered as soon as the phone started to ring.

"Have you seen her?"

"She hasn't left the house," Susannah said.

"You're sure? And no one has come around to see her since last night?"

"No one."

Nick stared at the back of the dead man's brown suit as he walked into the heart of the graveyard. *How? How did he get past me? How come Susannah didn't see him?* The only explanation was that the dead man had slipped between the cemetery gates while Nick was chasing Jane Hamilton away from the school-children. And Susannah? Maybe she had also been distracted, or more likely the dead man had come to the back of Abby's house. In truth it didn't matter – what had happened didn't change where they were now.

"Can you come and pick me up?" he asked.

"I can be there in twenty minutes," Susannah promised.

The street was quiet. Oppressive. Nothing moved. Abby's house squatted halfway down on the left-hand side. The curtains were closed, and Nick didn't need to get any closer to detect the sense of isolation and abandonment.

He ran from the car to Abby's house and Susannah followed. Nick banged his fist against the door. Even if she'd been asleep the noise was loud enough to wake her. *Loud enough to wake the dead*, Nick thought and redoubled his effort.

He crouched on the step so he was level with the letter box. He opened his mouth to call out to her, but when he breathed in, he stopped short. The air inside the house was thick and still, as if nothing had moved for days. When it hit the back of his throat it tasted sickly sweet, like a piece of meat left out in the sun for too long.

"Do you think we need to call Timothy?" Susannah asked. "He can be here in a few minutes."

"I have a key."

Nick put the key in the lock. It turned easily. When he opened the door he was aware of the woman close behind him; she took one lungful of the foul air inside the house and retched.

He headed straight upstairs and stood over Abby's bed. Susannah sidled quietly into the room and stood beside him. She said nothing, and for that Nick was grateful.

Abby's duvet was thrown off the bed. Nick remembered occasions when he had woken in the night and Abby had gathered all the bedding across from her. Looking at the bed it appeared that it was a trait she was equally prone to when she was sleeping alone.

There was a stain on the sheet; a yellow-white discharge about twice the size of Abby's head. Nick didn't know what it was – maybe dried blood or mucus or something – but he didn't want to think about it too deeply. What mattered was that the stain was there, but Abby was not. There was movement on the sheet; white upon white. He looked closer and saw the writhing action of maggots. Behind him, Susannah fled.

He moved to the bed and tried to ignore the maggots, but their motion drew his eye. On the sheet he saw tiny yellow-brown pupae cases.

Where's Abby?

He imagined her lying in this bed, the infection racing through her body. She died alone. For Nick, that was the worst aspect – not *that* she had died, not *how* she had died, but that she had died without anyone to hold her hand.

Susannah returned to the doorway. Her face was flushed, and the front of her hair was wet.

"Where is she?"

Nick shrugged. "How should I know?"

But as soon as he spoke he realised. Of course he knew. He pushed past Susannah and ran down the stairs.

CHAPTER 27

He stood on the cobblestones in the gateway and called out, "Abby!" A young couple turned to him and he expected them to shush him as if he were in a church.

"Abby!" he called again. A few of the dead were dotted around the cemetery and they glanced in his direction. He wanted to stride in and grab them; shake them until they told him where Abby was, but he was a coward left standing on the sidelines and staring in, his feet never crossing onto the smooth tarmac on the other side of the gates.

After ten minutes of shouting, he fell silent. If Abby was inside the cemetery, she would not heed his summons.

He stared through the railings at the graves beyond. The fencing did nothing to hold in the stink of the dead. It was stronger than he had experienced before, multi-layered, as if he was sensing the stench of each of the dead in the graveyard, separately and together. He concentrated and tried to decide if he could detect Abby. A smell that was only hers.

A family passed through the gates and Nick envied their easy movement. There were no stuttering steps on the edge of the graveyard, no fear-induced panic sweats on their brows. A mother and two children, both boys. The younger boy carried a bouquet of flowers and the mother bent down to say something to him. All three wore the fractured, tentative faces of the recently bereaved.

Nick imagined walking over the cobblestones and simply passing through the gates and into the cemetery.

He would go inside and find Abby and then... but he didn't manage to get that far. He took a single step and felt the heat flush through his body and the shakes rake his limbs. He crushed his hands into fists held down by his sides.

The gates were wide open, as if waiting to receive a hearse. Nick felt vulnerable at the lack of a barrier between him and the gravestones. Even the iron railings offered him some protection, but now there was nothing. The graveyard slipped down the hill so he could only see the first few hundred graves, but he could feel the others just out of sight. They pressed their weight against the air.

The gravestones around the entrance looked old – orange stone worn away so the inscriptions were too weathered to be read.

He *knew* Abby was inside the graveyard. He couldn't smell her or taste her or hear her or see her. He longed to touch her, but he knew that was something now forbidden. And yet despite all that he *knew* she was somewhere in the graveyard.

There was nothing stopping him from walking straight into the cemetery. Nothing at all. Except himself. He bit his lip until he felt tendrils of pain spreading out along his jawline. He tried to take a step forward and in his mind he actually covered the distance between the side of the road and the entrance to the graveyard in a flurry of steps. In reality, he stood as still as the stone angels which hung above the graves a few feet away from him.

Because he was afraid.

He wanted to cry, but tears would not come. Instead, he was left with a knot in his throat that stopped any breath he took. Abby would understand. She had understood when he had been unable to attend her mother's funeral, even though he had never been able to explain his reason.

Except that was crap, Nick thought. Of course, she wouldn't understand. She was in that graveyard waiting for him to come for her. He could feel her screaming out for him.

The family walked back up the hill, the child's arms now empty. Behind the family came two of the dead. Nick didn't recognise either of them but he could smell their scent on the wind. They followed the family like mourners trailing a funeral cortege.

"Leave me alone," he shouted. The mother stared at him and gathered her children closer to her side. She squeezed through the gate, shielding her children from him.

The two dead men stood on the other side of the cemetery, where the cobblestoned path gave way to tarmac. They grinned, a gap-toothed, decay-infested grin with earthworms writhing through their sparse hair and flakes of dead skin falling from their cheeks. *They need to feed soon.*

In the end he ran back across the street. Retreated into his cowardice.

CHAPTER 28

Nick sat in the doorway of a house on the far side of the road and waited. He watched visitors arriving and leaving the cemetery. A long black hearse slipped through the gates and headed down the path. During all this he watched the dead moving between the graves. Some of the figures he recognised; at one point he saw Jane Hamilton, the lad in the SuperDry hoodie, the woman with the blonde-straw hair. Others were familiar without being individual.

The sky darkened as the sun began to fade. His thin coat was no protection against the cold, no matter how tightly he wrapped it around him. But he waited.

He glanced away from the graveyard – along the columns of traffic that poured into the city centre. A figure snagged his attention. The man walked up the hill, bent double with the effort. At first Nick saw only the crown of his head – the thin white scalp and the tufts of grey hair. The man wore a thick winter coat, a piece of clothing that looked like it had served a Russian soldier in the First World War.

Nick looked back to the graveyard and continued his vigil.

The man stopped in front of him, blocking his view. Nick saw only thin legs, like a pair of saplings wrapped in denim. He looked up past the trench coat that flapped around the man's wiry shoulders, and into the face of the man.

Age hung on him as heavy as the coat. It was in the way he moved, the way he stood. It was in each harsh, laboured breath he took – a fifty cigarettes a day man with chronic emphysema. He smelled of dust and ointments.

His eyes were almost grey. The man stared out and took in the whole world with a mixture of knowledge and sadness.

Nick dropped his head to look past the man's spindly legs to the cemetery gates.

"Don't you recognise me?"

The voice was familiar. Nick looked back up at the man.

"Dad?"

The old man smiled, but it was an expression laced with pain.

Nick shuffled to make room on the step. He was aware of the thinness of his father's body pressed beside him, so slight he almost wasn't there. This close his father's breathing made a sharp whistling sound with each inhalation.

Nick searched for something to say but all his mind came up with were trite queries about the trip and the weather in Bristol. Instead, he was silent.

He could feel his father waiting for him to speak.

"You called me."

"You're too late."

Some of the cars coming up the hill had their side lights on. Not all of them, not yet, but the evening was encroaching. Shadows lengthened and parts of the cemetery were already shrouded in an early-evening gloom, as if night came early for the dead.

Shadows moved within the shadows. Some of the figures were visitors, making tributes to their lost. There was a preponderance of old women, bowed down under the weight of their handbags. They drifted through the gates and disappeared out of sight down the slope of the cemetery.

Most were visitors, but not all. Some of the shadows belonged there. They pressed against the darkness. They drifted between the graves. From his seat it was impossible to recognise any of the figures. They could have been male or female, young or old. Nick wanted to believe he would recognise Abby, but that was probably not the case.

"She's gone," Nick said. Until he said the words aloud, he hadn't realised he had been holding onto the belief that Abby was still alive. In his imagination he stormed the cemetery, confronted the dead, and stole Abby back.

Nick heard a soft, almost silent sound and he turned and looked at the man beside him. Much of his father's face was hidden by shadow, but now Nick was able to pick out hints of the man he remembered. It was something about the way he sat staring into the distance.

His father was crying. Silently. It occurred to Nick that he could probably ask any question he wanted and he would receive the answer: how his mother had died, why his father had abandoned him, maybe even what could be done about the dead. But he remained silent; he no longer needed answers.

He stood up. The traffic was lighter and crossing the road was easy. As they stood in front of the cemetery gates panic flooded through Nick. He was still afraid, but he would always be afraid.

He could smell petrol and diesel fumes. He could smell dead flowers lying in a dustbin on the other side of the gates, still in their plastic shrouds. He could smell the dead. All of the dead.

He started to turn, to flee. His father's thin fingers dug into his shoulder and stopped him.

"When your mother passed over, I never got the chance to say goodbye," his dad said. "You can't let the same thing happen to you." He held out his hand and Nick took it. The skin was soft and warm.

"We do this together," his father said, and took a step across the cobblestones and through the gates.

CHAPTER 29

Nick didn't breathe. He closed his eyes and felt every muscle in his body tense.

There was no crash of thunder or explosion of screams. There was no rush of the dead toward him as he trespassed on their ground. There was only the smooth tarmac beneath his feet replacing the uneven cobblestones. He opened his eyes and night flooded in. Nothing had changed. *Is this it?*

Nick felt his father's hand squeeze his own, almost crushing his fingers.

You are as frightened as I am, Nick thought.

From the main entrance the cemetery had two paths: one ran along the left, parallel to the iron fence, and the second plunged straight into the heart of the graveyard, winding between headstones and dropping out of sight.

He found himself imagining he was a child once more, with his dad towering over him, even though Nick could remember the pencil marks on the kitchen wall which tracked his height until he had overtaken both of his parents.

They walked between ornate gravestones carved with names and dates. Nick checked behind him; the open gates seemed miles away.

The path curved to the left and Nick followed. He noticed the dead drifting between the graves and wondered why they did not come closer.

The smell of wet earth rose up from the ground and coated the back of his throat.

The graves changed – no more Victorian crypts and avenging angels, now the small headstones were arranged in neat lines.

And still they went down.

"Your mother is here."

Nick turned quickly and looked behind him, but the path was empty. He peered beneath the trees and between the graves, and then he knew what his father meant. He felt a pang of disappointment. "Buried here?" he asked.

He felt his father nod.

"Where?

"I don't know. I've never been able to visit."

The hand that clasped Nick's clung ever more tightly.

As Nick passed the graves, he tried to read the names engraved on the headstones. It was an impossible task – the light was too poor.

"I tried," his father said. "I came back."

Nick tried to push away what that meant – that his father had been back here in the city, probably sitting on the same step opposite the graveyard, and had slipped away without contacting him.

"I never got to say goodbye," his father said. "I couldn't let you go through that."

Near the bottom of the cemetery all that was visible was the sheer cliffs which stretched around them. The path curved around a stone outcropping. The way ahead was barred with the dead. Thousands of the dead.

CHAPTER 30

They stood in silence. No scent. No motion. It was almost possible to believe they were statues.

Nick recognised some of those who stood before him. He saw two of the men that had walked through the Market Square the previous weekend. He saw Jimmy Miller who had died when he was seventeen – a child trapped in the body of a man. He saw faces he knew from newspaper reports over the years which had told of sudden deaths or long illnesses. He saw Jane Hamilton; near the front and standing as motionless as the rest.

"What do you want?" he asked them. There was no reply.

He saw Abby.

His heart stopped. For a long moment he couldn't breathe. *This is what death feels like*, but then his heartbeat returned, kicking his chest like a hammer crashing through his ribs.

Abby.

The disease had withered the left side of her body and her arm hung useless by her hips. Her beautiful face had been touched by the poison so it was now permanently in shadow.

He took a step forward. Abby gave no indication she noticed him. She did not look in his direction. She did not move.

Nick felt his father's hand grasp at his own, holding him back.

"It's time to say goodbye," his father whispered. The words were barely audible.

Nick disentangled his fingers from his father's. He heard the old man's words stutter as understanding came crashing in. "I... i... didn't bring you here for this."

"This is why I came," Nick said. He turned to face Abby. "You can feed from me."

He took a step closer. He thought he saw a faint smile flicker across Abby's lips.

"I'm not afraid of you," he said.

He could see where decay burrowed into her features, rotting the skin around her throat and turning it black. This close he could see the full destruction of her death. He pushed the image away and tried to remember her as she was before the dead man claimed her. How she would be once she had fed.

He reached out and pulled her into an embrace.

Epilogue

Mike Teel hesitated as he passed through the cemetery gates. From the corner of his eye he saw silhouettes drifting among the graves. He looked directly ahead and walked toward the centre of the cemetery, following the curve of the path round and down.

He stopped in front of a mausoleum of white marble stained with dirt. The engraving remembered Elijah and Helen Campbell who departed this earth in 1922 for Eternal Glory. From the Campbells' marker Mike struck out across the grass, winding between the plots. The first time it had taken him over an hour but now a badger track of downtrodden grass marked his earlier visits and he came upon the grave without having to detour.

The headstone was simple; a black marker with *Joanne Teel* engraved in gold writing. The empty space below his wife's name ached. It should commemorate her life. It should tell how she loved and was loved. She was so much more than the dates scratched into the surface of a stone.

Eventually he left the grave and returned to the path. He moved further into the cemetery where some of the graves were still mounds of black earth marked only by temporary wooden crosses. He did not raise his eyes from the ground but still he noticed the flickers of motion at the edge of his vision.

Nick's grave was too recent – the turned earth a brown scar on the ground. Mike sensed a presence behind him.

He wanted to turn and see Nick and Abby. Together. But he understood that would never happen. The boy was alone, that was the most terrible part of it. Despite everything, he was still alone.

Sometimes Mike found he almost understood what his son had done, but mostly he cursed the theft.

The marker over the grave read: *Nicholas Teel. Taken too soon.*

Mike stayed until darkness fell over the cemetery. Until the movement at the edge of his sight gathered together and formed a crowd around him. As he stood to leave, they formed a slim passage through which he could exit, and he tried not to think of the time when it would not happen.

THE END?

Not if you want to dive into more of Crystal Lake Publishing's Tales from the Darkest Depths!

Check out our amazing website and online store or download our latest catalog here.

https://geni.us/CLPCatalog

We always have great new projects and content on the website to dive into, as well as a newsletter, behind the scenes options, social media platforms, our own dark fiction shared-world series and our very own webstore. Our webstore even has categories specifically for KU books, non-fiction, anthologies, and of course more novels and novellas.

ABOUT THE AUTHOR

Richard Farren Barber was born in Nottingham in July 1970. After studying in London he returned to the East Midlands. He lives with his wife and son and works as a manager for a local university.

He's fairly confident people only read these bios to check the author isn't a serial killer. (Spoiler alert: he's not.)

He has over 80 short stories published, seven novellas: "The Power of Nothing", "The Sleeping Dead", "Odette", "Perfect Darkness, Perfect Silence", "Closer Still", "All Hell." , and "Twenty Years Dead." His two novels are: "The Living and the Lost" and "The Screaming Dead" (Co-authored with Peter Mark May).

If you want to check on his serial killer tendencies, follow him on twitter.com/rfarrenbarber and www.facebook.com/richardfarrenbarber

His website can be found here www.richardfarrenbarber.co.uk

Readers…

Thank you for reading *One of the Dead*. We hope you enjoyed this novella.

If you have a moment, please review *One of the Dead* at the store where you bought it.

Help other readers by telling them why you enjoyed this book. No need to write an in-depth discussion. Even a single sentence will be greatly appreciated. Reviews go a long way to helping a book sell, and is great for an author's career. It'll also help us to continue publishing quality books.

Thank you again for taking the time to journey with Crystal Lake Publishing.

You will find links to all our social media platforms on our Linktree page. https://linktr.ee/CrystalLakePublishing

Follow us on Amazon:

MISSION STATEMENT

Since its founding in August 2012, Crystal Lake Publishing has quickly become one of the world's leading publishers of Dark Fiction and Horror books. In 2023, Crystal Lake Publishing formed a part of Crystal Lake Entertainment, joining several other divisions, including Torrid Waters, Crystal Lake Comics, Crystal Lake Kids, and many more.

While we strive to present only the highest quality fiction and entertainment, we also endeavour to support authors along their writing journey. We offer our time and experience in non-fiction projects, as well as author mentoring and services, at competitive prices.

With several Bram Stoker Award wins and many other wins and nominations (including the HWA's Specialty Press Award), Crystal Lake Publishing puts integrity, honor, and respect at the forefront of our publishing operations.

We strive for each book and outreach program we spearhead to not only entertain and touch or comment on issues that affect our readers, but also to strengthen and support the Dark Fiction field and its authors.

Not only do we find and publish authors we believe are destined for greatness, but we strive to work with men and women who endeavour to be decent human beings who care more for others than themselves, while still being hard working, driven, and passionate artists and storytellers.

Crystal Lake Publishing is and will always be a beacon of what passion and dedication, combined with overwhelming teamwork and respect, can accomplish. We endeavour to know each and every one of our readers, while building personal relationships with our authors, reviewers, bloggers, podcasters, bookstores, and libraries.

We will be as trustworthy, forthright, and transparent as any business can be, while also keeping most of the headaches away from our authors, since it's our job to solve the problems so they can stay in a creative mind. Which of course also means paying our authors.

We do not just publish books, we present to you worlds within your world, doors within your mind, from talented authors who sacrifice so much for a moment of your time.

There are some amazing small presses out there, and through collaboration and open forums we will continue to support other presses in the goal of helping authors and showing the world what quality small presses are capable of accomplishing. No one wins when a small press goes down, so we will always be there to support hardworking, legitimate presses and their authors. We don't see Crystal Lake as the best press out there, but we will always strive to be the best, strive to be the most interactive and grateful, and even blessed press around. No matter what happens over time, we will also take our mission very seriously while appreciating where we are and enjoying the journey.

What do we offer our authors that they can't do for themselves through self-publishing?

We are big supporters of self-publishing (especially hybrid publishing), if done with care, patience, and planning. However, not every author has the time or inclination to do market research, advertise, and set up book launch strategies. Although a lot of authors are successful in doing it all, strong small presses will always be there for the authors who just want to do what they do best: write.

What we offer is experience, industry knowledge, contacts and trust built up over years. And due to our strong brand and trusting fanbase, every Crystal Lake Publishing book comes with weight of respect. In time our fans begin to trust our judgment and will try a new author purely based on our support of said author.

With each launch we strive to fine-tune our approach, learn from our mistakes, and increase our reach. We continue to assure our authors that we're here for them and that we'll carry the weight of the launch and dealing with third parties while they focus on their strengths—be it writing, interviews, blogs, signings, etc.

We also offer several mentoring packages to authors that include knowledge and skills they can use in both traditional and self-publishing endeavours.

We look forward to launching many new careers.

This is what we believe in. What we stand for. This will be our legacy.

Welcome to Crystal Lake Publishing—Tales from the Darkest Depths.